BEDTIME FURY

FEDERAL BUREAU OF MAGIC COZY MYSTERY, BOOK 5

ANNABEL CHASE

RED PALM PRESS LLC

CHAPTER ONE

PANCAKES SIZZLED ON THE GRIDDLE. I watched the rounded edges bubble and brown as I waited for the right moment to drop in a handful of blueberries.

"I want chocolate chip," she said.

Now you might think that 'she' refers to my five-year-old niece, Olivia, but you would be wrong.

"Grandma, I already told you I'm making blueberry pancakes," I said. "If you want chocolate chips in yours, then you'll have to make them yourself."

Grandma glared at me from the dining table. "I thought you were making us breakfast for a change."

I slid the spatula underneath the first pancake and flipped it. "Exactly. I said I'd make breakfast, not take orders. This isn't Gouda Nuff."

"It sure isn't," Grandma mumbled.

"Chocolate chip pancakes are dessert, not breakfast," Verity said from her place at the table. As a doctor, my sister-in-law is firmly entrenched in the minimum five fruits and vegetables per day camp.

"Dessert for breakfast!" Olivia cried out. "I can't wait to tell my teacher." She hopped up and down in her chair.

"Now sweetheart, there's no need to tell your teacher what you ate for breakfast," Verity said.

Despite the affectionate tone, I heard the unspoken panic that she would be judged for her poor choice to serve her daughter such an unhealthy morning meal. I don't envy moms today.

"Well, I have to tell Prudence," Olivia said. "She's always boasting about her muffin like it's a gift from the gods."

"Sounds like your grandmother," Grandma quipped, and Verity shot her a silencing look.

"You don't need to compete with Prudence," Verity said.

"Not when you're the clear winner," Grandma added.

Verity pressed her lips into a thin line. "That's not what I mean."

Olivia crossed her arms. "Prudence says she's better than me because the teacher gave her the Patience Award this month."

"It *is* a virtue," Verity said. "Especially for children."

"I'll teach you a spell that puts ants in her pants," Grandma told the five-year-old. "That'll put Prudence in her place."

"Esther, don't encourage her," Aunt Thora said.

"You're one to talk," Grandma said. "I seem to recall some of your more creative spells when a classmate annoyed you."

Olivia's blue eyes shone. "Like what?"

"I was young and foolish," Aunt Thora said.

"Liar, liar, pants on fire was inspired," Grandma countered.

"No one is setting anyone's pants on fire," Verity said firmly.

I flipped the rest of the pancakes and listened to the satisfying hiss as the batter hit the heat.

"Where's the coffee?" my mother's voice rang out. She sauntered into the kitchen, still in her pink silk robe and ballet-style slippers. Her hair and makeup, on the other hand, looked red carpet-ready.

"You literally just walked in here and you're already making demands," I said. "How about 'gosh, Eden, those pancakes sure smell good.'"

My mother splayed her hands on the countertop. "Coffee smells better. Now do you intend to make any or should I get it started?"

"Really the coffee should've been started first," Grandma said. "People always have their first cup before eating."

I groaned as I served the first batch of pancakes onto a plate. "Grandma, you always have tea when you first wake up."

Grandma wore an innocent expression. "I didn't say me. I said people."

"You know, Eden," my mother said, "if you ever expect to get married and have a family of your own, you need to learn how to do these things."

"Is that what this is, Eden?" Aunt Thora asked. "Are you practicing?"

I delivered a serving plate stacked with pancakes to the middle of the table. "The only reason I'm doing this is to be nice to my family."

"Oh, good," Grandma said. "You could use the practice."

I shot her a dark look before returning to the griddle for the next batch. In truth, I had an ulterior motive, but I wasn't about to share it. My secret hope was that I would kill my family with kindness so they would stop killing each other with lightning bolts. I wanted to appeal to the slivers of good in their natures and show them how nice it felt to give and receive kindness. I figured breakfast was a good place to start. It was, after all, the most important meal of the day.

"I, for one, appreciate Eden's efforts this morning," Verity said. "Aunt Thora, can you please pass the syrup?"

"We sure are going to miss having you here," Aunt Thora said.

"Speak for yourself," Grandma muttered.

"We all knew this day would come," Verity said. "Living with you was only ever meant to be temporary."

Now that the renovations on their house were finally finished, my brother and his family were moving out of my mother's house. I wasn't sure how much would really change, given that the children would still be here most days while their parents work and they decided to leave behind Charlemagne, their Burmese python. Their house was only five minutes away. I imagined the children riding their bikes to visit me in the barn when they were old enough. One of the main reasons I felt better about being forced to return to Chipping Cheddar was the fact that I could be a positive influence on my niece and nephew. That meant spending quality time with them as often as possible.

Anton breezed into the kitchen in his suit and tie. "I'm running late." He stopped short and sniffed the air. "Why don't I smell coffee?"

"Because you smell pancakes," I said.

"Your sister didn't make any," my mother said.

Anton's gaze alighted on the stack and he grinned. "I can get coffee on the way to work, but I can't get pancakes." He squeezed in between Grandma and Verity. "Grandma, you know the rules. No screens at the table, please."

Grandma glanced up from her phone. "What? I'm about to level up."

"Little Critters again?" Anton asked.

"What else?" Grandma held up her phone. "I'm so close to the top level. All I have to do is win the next battle."

"You're setting a bad example for the children," Verity

said. She inclined her head toward Olivia and one-year-old Ryan in the high chair.

"I'm showing them how to be a winner," Grandma said. "How is that bad? They're certainly not going to learn it from their parents."

"Hey!" Anton said. "Verity and I are both successful."

"Sure, at your jobs," Grandma said. "Who cares about that?"

"I do," Verity said. "I take my job very seriously."

"We know," my mother said with a pinched smile.

I delivered the rest of the pancakes to the table and sat down to enjoy them.

"Coffee?" my mother prompted. She held up an empty mug and I was tempted to bonk her on the head with it—except that wasn't within the parameters of Operation Kill Them With Kindness.

"I'll take care of the coffee," Aunt Thora said. "I'm sure Eden has to leave for work shortly."

"Not dressed like that she doesn't," my mother said.

I glanced down at my gray T-shirt. "What's wrong with this? It's got a cute cat on it."

"What isn't wrong with it?" my mother shot back. "It says *pet me and die.*"

"So what?" I said. "It's funny."

"It's off-putting to a man," my mother said. "Makes you seem frigid, like some kind of ice princess."

"Elsa!" Olivia said.

"Conceal, don't feel," Anton added with an amused grin.

"Is Elsa your favorite princess?" I asked. I'd only been back in Chipping Cheddar for a few months and was still getting to know my niece and nephew. I'd been living in San Francisco where I worked as an FBI agent, until an unfortunate incident forced me back to my hometown, the one place I thought I'd never settle.

Olivia pulled a face. "No way. It's Ursula."

"I don't know a Princess Ursula," I said. "Which story is she from?"

"The Little Mermaid," Olivia said. "She's not a princess. She's a sea witch."

I had no doubt that was my family's influence.

My mother wasn't ready to let go of the problematic T-shirt situation. "There are plenty of cat T-shirts that don't make it seem like you're determined to be alone for the rest of your life," my mother said. "I saw an adorable one just the other day that said *the snuggle is real*." She pointed at me. "You wear that and you're sending the right sort of message."

"That I like puns?" I asked.

My mother scowled. "No need to be a smartass."

"I come by it honestly," I replied in sticky sweet tone. *Kind over matter*, I reminded myself. It didn't matter what my family threw at me, I was determined to rise above it and lead the way to goodness by example—even if it killed me.

"How are your pancakes, Ryan?" Verity asked.

"Why are you letting him eat pancakes with his hands?" my mother asked.

"There's no syrup on them," my sister-in-law said.

My mother placed a hand on her chest. "No syrup? That's like sex without an orgasm."

Anton grabbed his forehead. "Mom, could you not? We're eating."

"And there are children present," Verity added. "Besides, he doesn't need the extra sugar."

"Oh, honey," my mother said, "everybody needs a little extra sugar every now and again. Like I said…"

Anton held up a hand. "We know what you said. Thanks for the insightful analogy."

"Such prudes at this table," my mother grumbled.

Aunt Thora brought over the coffee pot and filled my mother's mug. "Anyone else?"

"No time," Anton said. He'd gobbled down his pancakes in record time. "I'll see everyone tonight. It's back-to-back meetings today." He kissed his wife and children goodbye.

"What about the move?" Verity asked. "You're supposed to help supervise."

Anton grabbed his wallet from the counter and stuffed it into his back pocket. "You're a much better supervisor than I'll ever be. I trust you."

Verity's mouth opened to protest, but Anton was gone before she could eek out a word.

My mother heaved a regretful sigh. "So much like his father."

"Not really," Verity said. She carried her plate to the sink. "He's already shown he has better taste in women."

Grandma glanced up from her phone with a mischievous smile. "Someone's feeling liberated on moving day."

I made a quiet escape before I drew anyone's ire. Operation Kill Them With Kindness didn't mean offering myself as a sacrificial lamb. There were plenty of actual lambs in Chipping Cheddar for that.

CHAPTER TWO

ON MY WAY to the office, I passed by Magic Beans, the new coffee shop owned by my witchy rival, Corinne LeRoux. The shop was reopened now, having been temporarily closed due to contaminated coffee beans. I noticed a sign in the window that read *Coffee with a Cop, Today 9-10am.* My heart sank. Apparently, Corinne's relationship with the chief of police was going so well that they decided to work together in some capacity. So much for getting to the office on time. I pulled into the first parking spot I saw. Although I knew it was like scratching a scab, I couldn't resist going in.

I lingered on the pavement and stole a quick glimpse inside. My stomach jumped slightly, as it always did at the sight of Sawyer Fox. The police chief sat at a table with his back to the door, while his pug, Achilles, drank from a bowl at his feet. The chief was deep in conversation with an older gentleman I didn't recognize. Corinne smiled as she brought the old man a cup of coffee. I'd be smiling too if I were dating the sexiest, most handsome man in Chipping Cheddar. I tried to shrug off the mantle of jealousy that had settled on my shoulders. After all, I was the one to reject a relationship with him—not that I wanted to. I would have liked nothing more than to embark on a normal relationship with the chief. Dinners on the waterfront, picnics at the park with the dogs, snuggling under a blanket in front of the television late at night—the works. Life wasn't that kind to me, though. I was saddled with responsibilities that trumped my personal feelings and desires. I had to make peace with that. Somehow.

Finally, I steeled myself and opened the door. Corinne glanced up as I entered and I caught the subtle look of surprise on her face. She likely didn't expect me back after the borer demon incident, the aforementioned contaminated coffee bean situation.

"Good morning, Eden," she said. Her hair was in its natural state today, beautiful brown curls with threads of gold. Sometimes she straightened it, but today was not one of those days.

Chief Fox craned his neck to greet me. "Hey there, Agent Fury. You're here for Coffee with a Cop, aren't you?"

I approached the table, ignoring the whirlwind in my stomach. "Sure. Why not?"

"Eden, do you know Mr. Riggin?" Corinne asked. "He lives out near the Tasker farm, past Cheddar Gorge."

The older gentleman looked at me. "Please, call me Stuart."

"Nice to meet you, Stuart," I said. "I used to play in the fields at the Tasker farm. My brother and I even rode their horses without their permission sometimes."

"Eden Fury committed an intentional criminal act?" Chief Fox asked. He clucked his tongue. "And yet they accepted you into the FBI. How standards have changed."

"We were stupid kids," I said. "To be honest, I can't believe the Tasker farm is still there. It must be one of the last hold-outs." Chipping Cheddar, Maryland had once been acres of farmland owned by English Puritans with surnames like Bradford, Danforth, and Cawdrey. Some of the dairy farmers eventually turned to cheesemaking, kickstarting the town's love affair with cheese.

"It is," Stuart agreed. "My wife and I have dinner with the Taskers sometimes. Mary Tasker might be known for the best apple pie in town, but my wife makes the best fidget pie you've ever tasted."

"I love fidget pie," Corinne said. "It's got to have a strong cheddar cheese, though, or it's too bland."

"That's sort of why I'm here," Stuart said.

"Fidget pie?" I asked.

Stuart offered a sad smile. "My wife."

"Mrs. Riggin hasn't been herself lately, apparently," Corinne said. "She left a roast in the oven and nearly set the house on fire."

"She didn't even seem upset about it," Stuart said. "She just said 'these things happen,' like it was nothing."

"I can see why you'd be concerned," I said. "Has she been evaluated by a doctor?"

Stuart nodded. "Doc says she's in good shape for her age. Couldn't find anything amiss. I'm telling you, though, she's not my Shelley. All the light has gone out of her eyes. She's always been the warmest woman in a room. People always want to talk her ear off because they sense her compassion."

"But not lately?" I asked.

"Yesterday, I tripped going up the stairs and fell on my face," Stuart said. "Got this mark to show for it." He pointed to a small cut on his chin. "The old Shelley would have made a fuss over me. Made me a drink and brought me a compress and a Band-Aid."

"But not this Shelley?" I asked.

Stuart's gaze dropped to the table. "She didn't even bother

to ask if I was all right. She just kept shucking corn as though nothing had happened."

"I'm sorry to hear that," I said. "If this continues, maybe consider getting a second opinion. My sister-in-law is a doctor here in town—Verity Fury. She'd be happy to examine your wife."

"Thank you kindly," Stuart said. "A second opinion isn't a bad idea."

"Mr. Riggin initially sat down to tell me about a fox that's been terrorizing his chickens," Chief Fox said. "We got a bit off-topic."

"You keep chickens?" I asked, delighted. "I always liked the idea of fresh eggs."

Stuart clasped his hands on the table. "That's definitely one of the perks. The downside is coming out in the morning and finding one of your chickens brutally murdered. You get attached." His expression clouded over. "I take it pretty hard. Shelley did, too, before…" He trailed off, unable to complete the sentence.

"I'll be sure to send Deputy Guthrie around to check on the chickens," the chief said. "We look after all our residents, not just the human ones." He reached down to stroke Achilles' head.

Chief Fox had no idea how true his statement was. He was human and new to Chipping Cheddar. He didn't know about the supernatural world in plain sight. He certainly didn't know he was dating a witch. At least the LeRoux witches weren't wicked like the ones in my family.

Stuart scraped back his chair and took his coffee cup with him. "I appreciate that, Chief. I don't want to take up any more of your time. You've got other interested parties waiting." He smiled at me.

"Oh, she's not interested," the chief said, and we both blushed at the remark.

Stuart shuffled toward the door, still smiling.

"You're providing security detail for chickens now?" I asked in a teasing tone.

"Those chickens are defenseless," the chief said. "It's our job to protect those that can't protect themselves."

I couldn't resist a smile. "In that case, I have a few newts in my garden that need protection from my grandmother's cat." Candy was a relentless hunter. Grandma might be the one attacking Little Critters on her phone, but Candy was the real life culprit.

"Sounds like poor Shelley Riggin is in the early stages of dementia," Corinne said.

"I was thinking the same thing," Chief Fox said. "Poor guy. That's got to be rough."

"Corinne, we need you," the barista called from behind the counter.

Corinne flashed a bright smile. "Thanks so much for doing this, Sawyer. I think it's going really well." She hurried to the busy counter.

Not Chief Fox.

Sawyer.

I shoved the thought aside and slid into Mr. Riggin's vacant seat. "I bet you didn't expect Coffee with a Cop to end up as a therapy session."

The chief shrugged. "It's a community outreach program. If the guy wants to vent about his wife, then I'm here to listen." His pleasant expression faded. "Besides, I understand what he's going through."

"You do?"

The chief swilled his coffee. "My grandfather went through something similar. He developed dementia after my grandmother died and could never remember that she was gone. Each day was a fresh hell. We'd explain to him that she died—

cancer—but that didn't stop him from buying her birthday and anniversary cards and wondering why she never opened them. At one point, he assumed that she left him for another man because her clothes were gone." He raked a hand through his hair. "Man, I forgot how horrible that whole thing was."

"Where is he now?" I asked. "Iowa?"

"He was. He died about a year later." He inhaled deeply. "It was a blessing, really. Nobody should have to live like that, day in and day out, believing that the woman you loved didn't love you back."

"I'm so sorry," I said.

"I hope Mr. Riggin has better luck." He reached down to scratch Achilles behind the ear. "So what brings you in? Corinne said you'd be going back to The Daily Grind."

I stiffened. "She said that?"

"She did. She said she was sure that you preferred the coffee there and that she doubted you'd be a regular customer."

I wondered whether that was wishful thinking on her part. She knew the chief had been interested in me and that I shot him down before she swooped in. Did she suspect that my rejection wasn't genuine? Or did she just not like the idea of competition for the chief's affections? It was bad enough that our families were constantly at odds. I'd hoped that she and I could do better.

"I think a little competition is healthy," I said.

He grinned. "We are talking about coffee shops, right?"

"Of course. What else?" I fiddled with the strap of my handbag. "So how are things going between you two?"

"Nice and easy," he said. "Corinne's got a laid-back personality. Doesn't get caught up in nonsense. I like that about her."

"Have you met her family yet?" I asked.

"It's very casual, Fury," he said. "If I meet her family, it's because I need to issue them a parking ticket."

"You're lucky you don't have parents nearby breathing down your neck to get married."

He chuckled. "Thankfully not. Neither of us has marriage in mind. I'm still getting a handle on my job and she's got this place to run."

"Speaking of places to run, I need to get to the office before Neville sends out a search party." I looked wistfully at the counter, thinking of the delicious latte I'd enjoyed here, before it was discovered that the beans had been illegally imported from Otherworld. I wondered how the drinks tasted here now.

Corinne emerged from behind the counter, carrying a disposable cup. "You look like you're heading out." She thrust the cup into my hand. "One for the road."

I glanced at the cup in disbelief. "Really?"

"I added a dash of cinnamon," she said. "I seem to recall you like that."

"Thanks. I really appreciate it." I bent down to pet Achilles before I left and the playful pug licked my hand. "Nice to see you, Chief. Keep up the good work."

I scuttled from the shop before my emotions betrayed me. It was harder than I expected to see that their relationship was thriving, however 'casual.' It was even harder to have Corinne be nice to me despite our families' history. Maybe she'd think twice if she knew that I secretly coveted the man she was dating and had only rejected him for his own protection.

I left the pretty downtown area with its waterfront back-drop and crossed the railroad tracks into the seedier part of town on Asiago Street where my office was nestled between a donut shop and a tattoo parlor. Apparently, the Federal

Bureau of Magic wasn't willing to splurge for a view of the Chesapeake Bay.

I arrived at the office door, but was unable to open it. At first, I thought it was locked, until I realized that Neville had set up a new protective ward. My wizard assistant took his duties too far sometimes.

"Neville!" I yelled. "It's me! Open up!"

"How do I know who 'me' is?" he called.

I pulled out my phone, took a selfie in front of the door, and sent him a text with the photo attached.

"Still not convinced," he called.

"Who else would I be?"

"It could be an illusion," Neville said.

"Why would someone go to the trouble of crafting an illusion in order to access the office?" I asked. "Our computers aren't that interesting."

"There are other objects of interest in here," he said. "What's the secret word?"

I hesitated. "Did we come up with a secret word?" And was I drunk when it happened?

"Maybe we should."

I leaned against the door, losing patience. "Neville, I need to pee. Drop the ward right now or I'm going to go full fury on your…"

The door swung open and I fell forward, spilling part of my latte on the floor.

"It *is* you," Neville said cheerfully.

I scowled up at him before jumping to my feet. "I think maybe we should have a secret word to avoid these situations."

Neville scurried back to his desk as though I might punch him. "How about 'fury?'"

"Too obvious," I said. "We need something no one else could guess."

Neville scratched his chin, thinking. "Boston cream donut?"

"That's three words." I tossed my handbag on the desk and dropped into my chair. I rolled to the side and switched on my sun lamp, a gift from Chief Fox when he first moved to town. I was a big fan of natural light—something that was lacking in both my attic bedroom and the office. When I eventually moved into the barn that straddled my parents' properties, I'd have my fill of natural light, at least according to John Maclaren, the carpenter working on the renovation. He knew light was a priority for me.

"How about just donut?" Neville asked.

"That works," I agreed. "Anton and I used to have a secret word when we were kids."

"For what purpose?" Neville asked.

"Usually to let the other one know if our parents were on to us," I said. "It was the hint to change up our story or confess before we made things worse."

"What was the word?" Neville asked.

I stifled a laugh. "Mucus." We would find inventive ways to work the word into the conversation. Somehow, no one in the family caught on.

Neville wrinkled his nose. "You couldn't use a more pleasant term like 'bunny?'"

"My brother's a vengeance demon and I'm a fury," I said. "I think they got off easy with 'mucus.'"

"Fair point," Neville said.

I swiveled my chair toward him. "Have you gone through today's transmissions yet?" Every day, we receive notices from Otherworld that we need to review. Escaped demons, potential threats to the area, new guidelines. It's one of the main tasks required of our satellite FBM office. That, and check that the dormant portal to Otherworld located near Davenport Park isn't ready to bust open and spill dangerous supernatural creatures into this tranquil, primarily human town.

"Already finished the review, O' Majestic Goddess of Retribution."

I gave him a stern look. "I'm not majestic, a goddess, or in need of retribution."

"But you could be," he said. "It's in your nature."

I shuddered. "Let's not discuss my nature, please. You know how I feel about it." I hated every aspect of it, that's how I felt about it. If someone came to me tomorrow and said they could strip me of every fury trait I possessed, I'd empty my bank account. Take the wings. The immortality. The strength and speed. I would be more than happy to be a normal twenty-six year old woman with an annoying family and an excessive number of cat T-shirts.

He lifted a sheet of paper from his desk. "There's an arrest warrant for a demon in this world. Known smuggler. Location unknown. All offices are on alert."

"Show me."

Neville set the alert on my desk. "His name is Handel Gottsberg."

I examined the page. "Wait a minute. I know him. He's the distributor that Corinne used for the coffee beans, the ones imported from Otherworld. Her mother recommended him." No surprise that Rosalie LeRoux kept questionable company. Her antics didn't rise to the level of my family's, but her hands weren't exactly squeaky clean either.

"Any reason to think he'd come to Chipping Cheddar to see her?" Neville asked.

"Can't hurt to ask," I said.

Neville seemed unconvinced. "Isn't she the scary one in that coven?"

"Scary is probably an overstatement. She's not the most trustworthy LeRoux, let's put it that way." And she happened to have a small place a couple blocks away where she conned unsuspecting humans with her fake psychic abilities. Rosalie was a LeRoux witch with ties to New Orleans, but her psychic abilities were limited to knowing my family's opinion of her without needing to hear the words spoken.

"I'll accompany you then," Neville said. "No need for you to take one for the team."

"Why not?" I asked. "That's basically my specialty."

CHAPTER THREE

I STRODE into Rosalie's place with Neville practically stepping on my heels behind me. With clashing animal prints and
jewel-toned acrylic vessels scattered across every surface, the
interior was as tacky as its occupant. Corinne certainly
didn't get her eye for style from her mother.

"Hey there, Rosalie," I said.

She took a long drag on her cigarette before stubbing it
out in a paper cup on the table. "Well, well. Eden Fury. Say,
did you know they have entire conventions for your type?
Freaks."

I flinched. "Those aren't furies. Those are furries."

Rosalie inclined her head. "What's the difference?"

"The extra letter 'r,'" Neville said matter-of-factly.

Rosalie smirked. "I like this one."

Neville straightened. "Why, thank you."

"What do you need?" Rosalie asked. "Palm reading?" She
wiggled her fingers. "No charge."

"Funny," I said. "I'm looking for information on a friend
of yours."

Rosalie leaned back in her chair. "You'll have to be more specific. That's a pretty long list."

Neville held up the sheet of paper with Handel Gottsberg's image. With his hooked nose and sunken eyes, he wasn't the most attractive man on the planet. "This friend."

Rosalie arched an eyebrow. "Is this because of the borer demon? I thought we'd moved past that little snafu."

"I didn't issue the alert," I said. "This came from Otherworld." Although I had no doubt the FBM passed along details of Handel's involvement in the demon's appearance in town.

"He's a known smuggler," Neville said.

"Handel's a distributor," Rosalie insisted. "That's not a crime."

"It is when he distributes items from Otherworld."

"He sources hard-to-get items and distributes them." Her lips curved into a smile. "For a price, of course."

"Well, right now I'm a distributor," I said, tapping the page. "And I'm distributing his image so I can find him."

"Haven't seen him," Rosalie said. She picked up an emery board and began to file her nails. "Is that all?"

I inched closer and injected a pleading tone into my voice. "Rosalie, I'm really trying to bridge the gap between our families, so help a sister out. Tell me where I can find Handel."

"I would've thought my daughter's decision to date your beloved Chief Fox would wedge that gap wider than the Grand Canyon."

My stomach tightened. "Not at all. Corinne knows we're cool."

Rosalie cackled. "Like she needs your blessing. Chief Fox was more than happy to indulge her…interest."

Neville shot me a cautious look. "Perhaps we should stay on track."

My hands clenched into fists. "I'm not looking to cause trouble, Rosalie, but I'm authorized to use my powers to get you to comply."

Rosalie appeared impressed. "How about that? Sweet Eden Fury is finally turning sour. I wondered how long it would take to follow in your family's footsteps."

"I am *nothing* like them," I snarled.

Neville stepped between us. "Ms. LeRoux, I don't want to create drama here, but I have a weapon in my pocket and I'm not afraid to use it."

Rosalie glanced down at his trousers. "I hope you mean a banana."

Neville stuck his hand in his pocket. "One of my jobs is to make toys for Agent Fury to play with. Has she mentioned that?"

"Toys?" Rosalie repeated. She started to smile, but the expression on Neville's face seemed to make her think better of it. "Fine." She dropped the emery board. "Handel was here last week. We had lunch."

"What did he want?" I asked.

"To apologize for what happened," Rosalie said. "Whatever you might think of him, he felt terrible. He had no idea a borer demon had taken refuge in a coffee bean sack. He's not trying to cause trouble. He only wants to make his clients happy."

"He stopped by Chipping Cheddar to issue an apology?" I asked.

"That's right," Rosalie said. "Just because he's an alleged smuggler doesn't mean he's inconsiderate."

"I like that you felt the need to say alleged," I said. "I think everyone in this room has first-hand experience with his crime."

"Did he say where he was off to next?" Neville asked.

Rosalie tapped the emery board on the table. "He mentioned something about Nashville."

"Business or pleasure?" I asked.

Rosalie clucked her tongue. "Oh, Eden. So shortsighted of you to think it has to be one or the other. He might not be much to look at, but half his business model is being charming."

"Does he have any plans to return here?" I asked.

"If he does, he didn't share his plans with me," Rosalie said. "Does the FBM have a Nashville outpost?"

"You seem perfectly at ease with throwing a business associate under the bus," I said.

Rosalie shrugged. "It might surprise you to learn that I care about this town. Just because I don't run around with a badge doesn't mean I don't have its best interests at heart."

"In that case, why didn't you contact me when he came back to town?" I asked.

"Nice one," Neville whispered and elbowed me.

"I didn't realize anyone was looking for him or I would have," Rosalie said. "I know you're still relatively new to the job, but you might want to think about brushing up on your communication skills."

"Don't play ignorant with me," I said. "You knew he was responsible for bringing the borer demon to town. Common sense dictates that I'd be interested in speaking with him."

"Well, he was only here for an hour or so and he came unannounced," Rosalie said.

"Did he see anyone else while he was here?" I asked.

"After lunch, yes, but he didn't mention any names. His client list is confidential."

"I guess so, considering they engage his illegal services," I said.

Rosalie looked at me. "It's not any different from an

American tourist sneaking a bottle of wine in their suitcase after a visit to a French vineyard."

"Actually, it's a lot different," I said. "And if you can't see that, maybe you should ask your mother to explain." Adele LeRoux served on the local supernatural council with me and was a respected community leader. She had no interest in breaking the law.

Rosalie snorted. "I don't need any lessons from you, thanks. As far as this town is concerned, you're the loser that destroyed the world's biggest wheel of cheese."

"Which I used to trap the borer demon," I huffed, not that I could explain that to a town of unsuspecting humans.

Rosalie plucked another cigarette from inside her bra. "Any more questions before my mouth is otherwise engaged?"

Neville and I exchanged glances.

"No, I think we're done for now," I said, "but if you hear from Handel, I want you to contact me immediately."

She waved the hand with the cigarette. "Yes, yes. You'll be the first to know."

After our fruitless visit to question Rosalie, Neville and I headed to Davenport Park for a training session where I defeated three simulated demons and leveled up. It was like a real life version of Little Critters. If I weren't afraid of Grandma decimating half the town, I'd let her join in next time.

"Eden, honey, I am so glad you're home," my mother said, when I dragged my worn-out body home afterward. I had strength, stamina, and speed, but they didn't prevent sore and tired muscles.

"Since when?" I asked.

My mother offered a dismissive swat. "Don't be silly, sweetheart. You know we're all pleased to have you back."

I cast a suspicious look in her direction. Was she mocking my kindness plan?

"Do you want me to make dinner? Is that it?"

"No, no. Breakfast was quite enough for one day. I imagine that was taxing for you considering that you don't normally cook for anyone."

"I cooked for myself for years," I said. "How do you think I managed to eat all this time?"

"Oh, honey. Sticking a lonely dinner for one into the microwave doesn't count as cooking. Everybody knows that."

I folded my arms. "Just because I didn't become a master chef like Rafael doesn't mean I don't know how to cook." My cousin Rafael is the owner and head chef at Chophouse, the best restaurant in town. He elevates slicing and dicing to an art form.

"Once the barn is fully renovated, you'll be able to practice cooking to your heart's content," my mother said. She squeezed my cheek. "Then you might finally be good at it."

I ground my teeth in an effort not to respond.

"I should probably mention that it's time for the annual photo," my mother continued. "You'll actually be able to participate this year, now that you're back in town. Isn't that wonderful?"

I scrunched my nose. "Photo? What photo?" It took me a moment to process. "No, not that photo."

"Yes, that photo, and don't you dare try to wriggle out of it," my mother said. "You don't have the excuse of being thousands of miles away anymore."

"I can have my friend Cecily make you a new outfit," Aunt Thora piped up from her place at the kitchen counter.

"That's a good idea," my mother said. She proceeded to

24

scrutinize me. "There's no way Eden will still fit into the last outfit she wore."

"Hey!" I objected. "I might still be able to fit into it." Not that I wanted to. The Day of Darkness is basically Christmas for black magic witches and wizards. Gifts are exchanged and commemorative photos are taken and sent to family and friends. I'd been a reluctant participant as a child, but I saw no need to continue the tradition as an adult.

"Now that you mention it, Beatrice, I'm not so sure you'll fit into last year's outfit," Grandma said, shuffling into the room. She wore a black T-shirt that read—*What Doesn't Kill You Disappoints Me*. A little too on the nose, that one.

My mother turned to glare at her. "What are you suggesting?"

Grandma continued to the table, ignoring my mother's dagger eyes. "I'm suggesting that you've been displaying the same shortcomings with food that you do with men—an inability to say no."

My mother pursed her lips, and I could tell she was debating whether to escalate this conversation or let it go. "Well, I will have you know that I've decided to change things up this year anyway. I was going to suggest a new look for this year's photo."

Grandma arched a skeptical eyebrow. "What kind of new look and why is this the first I'm hearing about it?"

My mother sauntered over to the table and took a seat. "Well, we always go with black dresses and hats."

"Because it's traditional," Grandma said. "What do you think we should wear—Kelly green? We're not leprechauns celebrating St. Patrick's Day. Our holidays are real."

"I know that," my mother said. "It's just that I saw Khrystine Hepplewhite's photo from last year and their coven managed to look both frightening and sexy at the same time. If they can manage it, why can't we?"

"Because you won't be swapping the women, just the clothes," I said.

"I took the liberty of creating a few sketches," my mother said, ignoring me. "I'll go get them now, shall I? If Eden is joining us this year, we need to take that into account."

"I'm not so sure that I should," I said. "Technically, I'm not a witch. Besides, I'm an agent for the Federal Bureau of Magic now. I don't know that it would be appropriate to celebrate the Day of Darkness." That would be like working as an Agent of SHIELD and celebrating Hydra Day.

"Oh, Eden, you take everything so seriously," my mother said. "When will you learn to lighten up?"

"And when you do, start with those hairs under your chin," Grandma said. "I have a bleaching potion that works wonders."

I absently touched the skin beneath my chin. "I don't think I'm being overly sensitive," I said. "I have to believe that the FBM frowns upon a celebration of dark magic."

"It's more than a celebration," my mother said. "It's one of the most special days of the year. You can feel the energy."

"Exactly why I prefer to avoid it."

"Who's going to tell if you participate?" Grandma asked. "That midget you work with certainly isn't going to open his pie hole. He worships the ground you walk on."

"Neville is not a midget," I said. "He's a wizard and he's my assistant."

"And you're a fury, as well as a member of this family," my mother said heatedly. "If we're taking a family photo for a special day, then you're going to be in it and that's the end of the discussion."

"In that case, why not include Verity and Olivia?" I asked. "They're members of this family, too."

My mother gave me a cross look. "You know perfectly

well that Verity is a druid and a member of this family by marriage only."

"Then what about Olivia?" I asked.

My mother fell silent.

"She tried to wrangle Olivia, but Verity put her foot down and said no," Grandma said.

"She said it's because Olivia isn't a witch," my mother said, visibly annoyed, "but I know it's because she doesn't want Olivia to be part of something that Verity isn't. Selfish woman."

"Speaking of Verity, shouldn't she be here supervising the move?" I asked. There was no sign of boxes or suitcases.

"They finished here about two hours ago," my mother said. "Most of their belongings were in storage anyway."

"Well, I think Verity is right," I said.

My mother rolled her eyes. "Of course you do. Verity could say that gruyere is the best cheese and you'd agree with her."

"That's because gruyere is the best cheese," Aunt Thora chimed in.

"Olivia hasn't developed enough abilities yet to know where she falls on the supernatural spectrum," I said. Although there'd been some hints already, my niece was only five. It could take a few more years to know for certain, especially when dealing with a hybrid like her.

"The photo has been the three of you for years," I said. "There's no reason to start including me again now."

My mother stomped her foot like a petulant child. "Eden Joy Fury, as your mother, I command you to participate fully in the Day of Darkness."

"You command me? What's this really about?" I asked. "Why is this so important to you?"

"I know why," Grandma said. "Because in that same photo

she saw of the Hepplewhites in their new outfits, they were also celebrating a new marriage and a third grandchild."

Ah. Now I understood. "This is the wicked witches version of keeping up with the Joneses," I said. "Forget it. I'm not helping you puff up your numbers for the sake of appearances."

My mother crumpled. "It's bad enough that you eschew our traditions, but then you come back here unmarried and without any babies." She threw out her arms. "I'm the laughingstock of the Mid-Atlantic Chapter of Black Magic Babes."

"Newsflash, Mom. It isn't my job to make you feel good about yourself. That's your job and only your job." Before their divorce, one of my parents' repetitive arguments involved my father's inability to make her happy. Once he recognized his efforts were in vain, he stopped trying and that was the beginning of the end for their marriage.

"Don't you try to use that head voodoo on me," my mother simmered.

"Good luck with your photo shoot," I said. "I look forward to seeing the new outfits." I turned to retreat the attic.

"You think you're such a big shot now that you're an FBM agent," my mother said. "Need I remind you where the real power is in this town?"

Slowly, I turned back to look at her. "I am well aware of where the real power is, which is exactly why my job is so important."

"And yet you had no problem dipping into the well of dark magic when it suited you," my mother accused. "Our magic that you so despise. I saved this town on more than one occasion using that very magic that repulses you."

"Yes, but not because you willingly stepped up to help out of the goodness of your heart," I said. "Everything you do is for your own selfish purposes. Using your magic is always a last resort for me." So much for Operation Kindness.

My mother's cheeks reddened. "If it weren't for our magic, you wouldn't be half the fury you are now."

"Exactly. I'm glad you're finally starting to get it." I ran up the steps to the attic before anyone could stop me. My family refused to understand my position. It baffled them that I could reject the powers offered to me. I had learned over the years that it wasn't my job to explain it to them. Not that it was easy to bite my tongue all the time, but I had to accept that *they* weren't willing to accept *me*. For whatever reason, they remained under the misguided belief that they could nag me into submission.

Alice Wentworth hovered at the top of the stairs. The ghost's family was the previous owners of the farm my parents' houses were built on. My future home in the backyard had once been the barn that housed their farm animals.

"I've seen the outfits they wore last year," the ghost said. "Consider yourself lucky to have escaped."

"Oh, I do. I can only imagine what my mother's idea of sexy and frightening looks like."

"Your brother and Verity have moved out," Alice said. "Time for another transition."

"I'm sure they're looking forward to privacy again." There certainly wasn't much of that in this house.

"They have two small children," Alice said. "I don't think they'll have privacy for another sixteen years."

I laughed and stopped abruptly at the sound of someone screaming. "What on earth…?"

Alice floated over to the television. "Oops, sorry about that. I've been trying to break out of my comfort zone by trying horror movies. I figure what's to be afraid of now that I'm a ghost, right?"

I crossed the attic to my mattress and plopped down to take off my sweaty shoes. "You know I'm not a fan."

"I remember. Your family used to taunt you for it. They couldn't imagine that someone as powerful as a fury could be afraid of a child's rotating head that spewed pea soup."

"Have I mentioned they're very supportive?" I asked wryly. And right now, my mother was very angry. Probably best to avoid her until she calmed down. "I'm going to nap. Can you let me know when Aunt Thora's made dinner?" I'd use my invisibility locket and sneak down for food later.

"So much for Operation Kindness," Alice said.

"You left out the 'kill them' part." I sprawled across the mattress and fluffed the pillow. "It won't happen overnight," I replied. Truthfully, I knew winning them over to the good side might not happen at all, but it was worth a try —wasn't it?

CHAPTER FOUR

I MUST'VE BEEN MORE exhausted from training than I realized because I slept right through dinner and into the next morning. I woke up feeling strange. When I lifted my head off the pillow, it felt like a ten-pound weight had been attached to my head like a bow. I dragged myself into a seated position and touched my face.

"What on earth…?"

My skin felt rubbery and misshapen. Even worse, I could scarcely see the attic. My fingertips pressed the skin around my eyes. Everything felt puffy.

Alice emerged from a wall. She took one look at me and recoiled. "Eden!" she yelled. "There's a pumpkin demon in your bed!"

"There's a pumpkin demon?" I asked.

Alice peered at me. "Eden?"

I waved. "It's me. Something's going on."

Alice drifted forward. "What's the matter with your face?"

"I don't know," I said. "Why did you call me a pumpkin demon?"

"Because your head looks like a pumpkin."

Simple enough. "I need a mirror." That meant a trip to the bathroom downstairs. I worried about my equilibrium now that my head weighed more than it should. "Is it actually orange?"

She shook her head. "It's your head, only enlarged."

My head was too big. Great balls of a minotaur. I had a feeling I knew exactly what this was.

"Alice, did you notice anyone come up to the attic while I was asleep?"

Alice appeared thoughtful. "Not that I recall. There was you, of course. Oh, and your mother came up with clean laundry, but that's it."

"My mother came up with laundry?" I didn't wait for a response. I rooted around in search of evidence. I found it under the mattress—a Buffy the Vampire Slayer bobblehead tied to a bag of herbs with a mandrake root attached.

"Did your mother bring you a gift as a peace offering?" Alice asked.

"Not quite." I snatched the curse and ran downstairs to confront my mother, careful not to tip over on the way down.

I found her in the office on the computer.

"You know, some parents leave money from the tooth fairy under their children's pillows."

"It wasn't under your pillow. It was under the mattress." My mother swiveled around in the chair. She took one look at me and burst into laughter. "I'm surprised you managed to make it down from the attic without toppling over."

My arm jerked to my side. "Weebles wobble but they don't fall down."

Grandma appeared behind me. "What's going on?"

I turned around to face my mother's accomplice. There was no way Beatrice Fury acted alone. I didn't even manage to get a word out before my grandmother's cackle pierced my eardrum. "How about that? A physical manifestation of your ego."

"This isn't funny," I said. "I have to leave the house to go to work. How am I supposed to explain this to people?"

"Just tell them that your job has gone to your head," my mother said sweetly.

"I think it's obvious," Grandma said.

"Fix this, Mom," I insisted.

"Now, sweetheart," my mother said. "Try not to raise your blood pressure too high or you'll end up looking like a ripe tomato."

"The two of you are on my list," I said. I pushed past Grandma and fled to the bathroom for a better look.

"Ha! The only list you have is for the grocery store," my mother called after me.

It wasn't easy to see my reflection because my eyes were almost slits. I couldn't even see the immortal flames that now graced my irises.

"This is unbelievable," I muttered.

Aunt Thora appeared in the doorway. "Oh, my," she said when she saw me. "I was hoping they wouldn't actually go through with it."

"You could have stopped them," I said, but the moment the words were out of my mouth, I knew how ridiculous they sounded. Together, my mother and grandmother were an unstoppable force. Aunt Thora didn't stand a chance.

"I'm sorry, Eden," she said. "Why don't I see if I can find a spell to reverse it?"

"I would appreciate that," I said. "I have to go to the office."

"If you like, I can drive you there and drop you off at the door so no one sees you."

"Let's see what you come up with first," I said. "If we can reverse this before I leave the house, that would be best."

I decided to get my shower and get dressed. It was a little tricky washing my hair because my head kept bouncing off the walls of the shower stall. I had no sense of space with my enlarged head.

By the time I was ready to go, Aunt Thora had gone through her grimoire. I could tell by her expression that the news wasn't good.

"Give it to me straight," I said. I stood across the island from her in the kitchen."

"How about a nice cup of tea with lemon?" Aunt Thora offered.

"That bad, huh?" I asked. "I'm not sure I can eat or drink anything in this condition. I'm not even sure where my lips are."

"They do look nice," my mother said, now on the sofa in the family room. "Very plump like Angelina Jolie. You ought to consider keeping them."

My fingers brushed over my puffy lips. "No thank you."

"It looks like this spell is locked in," Aunt Thora said with a note of sympathy.

My heart jolted. "What do you mean by locked in?"

"It's the kind of curse on a timer," Aunt Thora said. "You just have to wait for it to run its course."

"We're not novices, unlike some FBM agents in town," Grandma said. She passed straight by me to fill the kettle with water.

I splayed my hands on the countertop. "And how long is this timer?"

"According to the grimoire, the curse lasts for twenty-four hours from the time it began."

So whenever my mother brought the laundry. "I'm going to kill both of them!"

"I'd like to see you try," Grandma said. Her attention was

back on her phone. "I caught two critters this morning and I haven't even left the house yet. That's a good day."

I lurched forward and nearly lost my balance in the process. I would have to remember to move slowly until my head was back to its normal size.

"You cannot curse people willy-nilly like this," I said.

"I would curse someone just for using the phrase willy-nilly," Grandma shot back. "You're not the boss of me and you never will be. I don't care how many badges you pin to your body."

"I can't believe this is all because I didn't want to take the Day of Darkness photo," I said. "The punishment seems disproportionate to the alleged crime."

"I don't mind driving you into town," Aunt Thora said.

"Eden would never go into town looking like someone filled her head with helium," my mother said. "She's too vain."

"I'm vain?" I echoed. "Who's the woman that refused to wear a hospital gown when she got her tonsils out because it made you look fat."

"It added at least ten pounds," my mother snapped. "It wasn't remotely flattering. And the color was dreadful."

I felt my resolve strengthen. I wasn't going to let their shenanigans pull me down. "You know what? You're not going to win this time. I'm going to go about my day like any other."

Grandma snickered. "Good luck with that." She shuffled back to her room.

Princess Buttercup, my beloved hellhound, bounded into the room and whimpered at the sight of me.

"I know," I said. "I'm sorry. I'll be back to normal tomorrow." I grabbed my keys and handbag from the counter. "I'm going to work now. I suggest staying out of my way for the next twenty-four hours."

I went to the car in the driveway and opened the door. It

wasn't easy to maneuver myself into the driver seat. I banged the top of my head twice on the way in. I managed to start the car, but before I could reverse out of the driveway, a knock on the window startled me. Mrs. Paulson stood next to the car in a powder pink jogging suit. I rolled down the window to greet my elderly neighbor.

"Good morning, Mrs. Paulson. Is everything okay?"

Her eyes popped at the sight of me. She seemed unable to form words. "What... You look..."

"I guess you're talking about my face," I said. "It's an allergic reaction. I'm heading to the doctor's now for a steroid solution. It should be back to normal tomorrow."

Mrs. Paulson breathed a sigh of relief, but I noticed that she maintained a safe distance. "I just came by to ask if your aunt's lemon trees have improved."

Aunt Thora's lemon trees and Mrs. Paulson's cabbages had both been affected by the borer demon.

"Much better, thank you," I said. "And your cabbages?"

"Back to normal," she replied. "I hope your head does the same."

I tried to smile, but my puffy lips made it awkward. "Thanks."

I backed out of the driveway and drove into town.

I needed to do my daily check on the portal, so I parked as close to the hill as possible. If I could keep the number of people seeing my bobblehead to a bare minimum, I'd consider it a success. My mistake was failing to check my surroundings before opening the car door.

"Agent Fury?"

I whirled around and nearly lost my balance. "Chief?"

His eyes widened when he got a better look at me.

Achilles's reaction was even worse. The pug dropped to the ground, rolled over, and played dead.

"I had an allergic reaction," I blurted.

"To what?" he asked, once he'd recovered his power of speech.

"Shampoo," I lied. I almost said 'hair color,' but then I didn't want him to think that my hair was really gray and picture me as an old lady.

"I've never heard of anyone being allergic to shampoo," the chief said.

"It was an organic brand I'd never tried before," I said. "I'm allergic to one of the ingredients."

"I'm sorry this happened to you." His expression reflected concern and a hint of something else—revulsion? Right now, I was so mortified that I wanted to open the dormant portal just so I could run through it and never return.

"It should clear up by tomorrow," I said. Assuming my family was to be believed.

"That's good," the chief said. He seemed to notice the pug's position for the first time. "Achilles, what are you doing?"

The pug rolled back to his feet and barked.

"I frightened him," I said.

"He's being silly, that's all," the chief said. "The more often we patrol, the more tricks he learns. People have started to carry treats in their pockets in case they run into us."

"That's sweet," I said. I doubt they'd do that for Princess Buttercup. She was too intimidating in her Great Dane form. I could only imagine how people would react if they saw her true form. My hellhound and I had more in common than I realized.

"Do you want to get the dogs together when you're less… bloated?" the chief asked.

Inwardly, I cringed. The chief would never forget the image of my enormous head. Maybe it was for the best.

"That would be nice," I said. "Why don't you check with Corinne and let me know when you're both available?"

"She's pretty busy with Magic Beans," he replied.

"Still, she might want to join us." *Mostly so she doesn't think I'm trying to insert myself into their relationship.*

Chief Fox saw right through me. "Agent Fury, you and I are friends, aren't we? And Corinne and I...Like I told you, it's very casual. If I want to spend time with another woman or ten other women, it's perfectly acceptable."

Ten other women? Underwear model abs or not, that was pushing his luck. "Trust me, Chief. You do not want to scorn a LeRoux."

He waved his hands. "There'll be no scorning. Promise."

"Have you kissed her?" I slapped my hand over my mouth. Why did I ask a question I most certainly did not want to know the answer to? Of course they'd kissed. They were single adults. Let's face it, he and I had kissed and we weren't even dating.

The chief chuckled. "For someone not interested in me, you sure seem interested in the particulars of my personal life."

My chest tightened. "Our jobs, Chief..."

He didn't let me finish. "I know, I know. You don't have to explain again. I'm only giving you a hard time because I like your expression when you're annoyed and frustrated. It's cute." He cocked his head. "Well, maybe not today with that oversized noggin."

"Way to make me feel self-conscious."

"What are you doing out here anyway?" he asked.

"Stretching my legs," I said. "Verity said fresh air would help reduce the swelling faster."

"You should walk along the promenade. Better views there."

"I might. I thought I'd start here at the park."

"Too bad you didn't bring Princess Buttercup."

"I came straight from the office," I lied. "I should probably take that walk now, so I can get back." As much as I wanted to keep talking to Chief Fox, I didn't want this enlarged version of me to show up in his nightmare tonight. The sooner he forgot, the better.

The chief seemed disappointed. "I need to get back and do some paperwork. My least favorite part of the job."

"Same," I said. "I'd much rather be out in the field." As far as the chief knew, I made a living fighting cybercrime. "But somebody's got to stop ransomware in its tracks."

"Shoot me a text when you have a date in mind…for the dogs," he added hastily.

"I will." I continued to stand there awkwardly until he and Achilles disappeared around the curve of the sidewalk. Then I dashed to the mound and took a quick look around before slipping inside.

The portal pulsed as I approached it. The fact that it was dormant didn't stop it from spewing magical energy. I checked for any changes. It was always a relief to find nothing noteworthy. If a day came when that changed, I had no idea what I'd do, other than call FBM headquarters in a panic. My office needed a red button to hit in an emergency. If the portal ever became active again, Chipping Cheddar was doomed.

"We need a contingency plan," I told Neville, upon arriving at the office.

The wizard looked up from his phone screen. "In case your head never shrinks?" I'd warned him about the curse in advance so that he didn't freak out when he saw me. I didn't need my morale crushed any further today.

"No," I said. "In case the portal ever reopens."

"Oh, my. Have I not shown you that?"

"Shown me what?"

He opened the drawer of his desk and rifled through the contents until he found what he was searching for. He walked over and dropped a red booklet on my desk.

"You made me read hundreds of pages of guidelines about trivial matters like not leaving the lights on overnight and costing the FBM money, but you forgot to show me *this*?"

Neville grimaced. "When you say it like that, it does seem like quite the oversight."

I opened the booklet and scanned the pages. "Have you read this?"

"Of course. Ages ago."

"So long ago that you've forgotten the emergency protocol?"

Neville scratched his head. "Um, no. Of course not. How could I? It's the main reason we have a satellite office in Chipping Cheddar."

"You're stalling while you try to remember, aren't you?"

His finger jerked in the air. "We have to alert the section chief at headquarters. That's first."

"How?"

"With a…phone?" he offered weakly.

"Is there an emergency contact number?" I asked. "What if it's after office hours?" Of course it would happen after office hours. When else would a catastrophe occur?

"You should familiarize yourself with the booklet."

I gave him a pointed look. "Sounds like you should, too." I skimmed the contents. "There are measures we have to take."

"Like what?"

"Evacuation." It was a last resort, but if demons started

pouring out of the portal, then evacuation was the only option.

Neville's cheek twitched. "It's highly unlikely."

"Agreed, but it's something we should discuss every so often," I said. "Run through a drill in the event we have to actually do it." I paused. "It's a shame the FBM doesn't bring the mayor into the fold. Her help would be invaluable in a crisis."

"Depends on who the mayor is during an emergency," Neville said. "Yes, Mayor Whitehead would probably make a wonderful ally, but what about her successor? If we make it official, we could end up hexing ourselves in the foot."

"You're right, Neville. I hadn't really thought about it that way." I paged through the booklet. "Still, if there was a way of bringing Mayor Whitehead in without making it official…"

Neville slapped the booklet closed. "She's a human, Agent Fury. It would be as damaging as telling the chief."

"But why do we think that?" I spun the chair to face him fully. "Do we not trust them? Do we think they're so weak that they'll crumble?"

"It's for their safety, too," Neville said.

"You sound like my family," I grumbled.

"The supernatural council exists for a reason," Neville said. "We exist for a reason. We don't need to draw in law enforcement or the local government."

"Unless there's a crisis that requires evacuation."

Neville blew air from his nostrils. "Preparation is the key to success. Familiarize yourself with the procedure and I'll do the same." He patted my shoulder. "I wouldn't worry too much about it, though. Agent Pidcock used to say that the odds of a dormant portal reopening were less than the return of the dinosaurs."

I arched an eyebrow. "Had he seen Jurassic Park? That science is solid."

He returned to his desk. "Any leads on the other client Handel visited when he was in town?"

"Not yet. I've been too busy having my head blown up the size of the Hindenburg." I drummed my fingernails on the desk. "Do you think we should leave a listening device in Rosalie's office?" Part of me didn't want to be privy to any sounds emanating from her place, no matter how useful.

"I considered it, but, as a witch, I worried she might be able to detect any magical items I left behind."

"Good point." And I didn't want to be on her bad side. "I guess I could ask Corinne if she has any ideas. She's had direct contact with Handel, too."

"You'll wait until your head is back to normal, won't you?" Neville asked. "No reason to give her customers a fright when she only recently reopened."

"Fair enough." I didn't want to leave it too long, though. If the mystery client knew more about Handel's travel plans, we might be able to track him.

A cat's meow emanated from my phone.

"What on earth is that?" Neville asked.

"A text from Clara." Clara Riley had been my best friend all the way through high school until I left for college and then the FBI. We'd drifted apart, mainly because I was determined to keep my distance from all things Chipping Cheddar. Obviously, that didn't work out quite the way I planned.

I quickly scanned the text. "Double-decker crap sandwich. I forgot I told Clara I'd meet her at the diner."

"You could always cancel," Neville said. "She'd understand if you told her…what happened."

Clara knew the truth about my family and wouldn't be surprised in the least to learn that my own mother had hexed me.

"No, I said I wouldn't let my family get the better of me today and that means sticking to my plans." Unfortunately,

42

Sassy was with her, which meant my former high school nemesis would get a close-up view of my swollen head.

I squared my shoulders and steeled my pride against any impending attacks. If there was one thing I knew, it was that big-headed girls don't cry.

CHAPTER FIVE

A SMALL GROUP was assembled outside Gouda Nuff when I arrived, and I immediately recognized the white head in the middle.

"Grandma, what are you doing here?"

"I should ask you the same thing," Grandma said, motioning to my head. "You shouldn't be allowed outside looking like that. You're scaring the children."

I reeled back. "You're the one scaring the children. Look at them. They're too frightened to say anything."

One little blond boy had tears in his eyes. "She always wins the battles. I'm never going to win one if she keeps playing."

"You're playing Little Critters again?" I asked.

Grandma hunched over and glared at the boy. "I have every right to be here, same as you. If you don't like it, go battle somewhere else."

"Go get a job," one of the older boys said. "Then you won't have so much time to play our games."

"I'm over eighty years old, you little punk," Grandma said. "What kind of a job do you suggest I get? Lumberjack?"

"That's not a job," the blond boy said. "That's a lifestyle."

A teenaged boy was fixated on me. "If I stick a pin in your head, will it deflate?" he finally asked.

"Seems to me there's already a leak," I said. "All I feel right now is hot air."

The teenager frowned. "I can tell that's an insult, but I'm not sure why."

"Shouldn't you all be in school?" I asked.

"It's lunchtime," the teenager said, as though that explained it.

Grandma gave a triumphant cry and the children moaned.

"What just happened?" I asked.

"I pulled a diffee on them while they were distracted by your big head," Grandma said with a note of pride.

"A diffee?" I repeated.

"It means she got one over on us," the teenager said. "Dude, don't be ignorant. Use the urban dictionary like everybody else."

"She won again," a little girl whimpered.

Grandma leaned down to address her. "This is life, kid," she said. "Not everybody gets a trophy." She held up her phone, victorious. "But this witch is undefeated…"

"You really are a witch, aren't you?" the little girl said.

"You have no idea," I murmured. I escaped the crowd and entered the diner, where I ran smack into Deputy Sean Guthrie.

"Oh, terrific," I grumbled. There were days when this town reminded me of an obstacle course and this was one of them.

The freckled redhead took one look at my bulbous head and I braced myself for the onslaught of insults. Sean and I had attended high school together but we'd never been friends, unless you counted a continuous exchange of barbed comments as a friendship.

"Are you okay, Eden?" he asked.

I laughed. "You're even becoming lazy with your insults. At least compare me to the moon or something."

His brow creased as he continued to examine me. "Does it hurt?" He reached out to touch my head and I smacked his hand away.

"It'll be fine by tomorrow," I said. No need to explain.

"That's good news," he said, though his voice was flat.

"Are *you* okay?" I asked.

"Life is good," he said. "Take care, Eden." He continued past me and out the door.

I stared after him for a moment, unsure what to think.

Sassy caught my eye from a corner booth and waved. If you'd told me a year ago that I'd be voluntarily socializing with Sassafras "Sassy" Persimmons, I would've said you were on the brink of a mental breakdown. Sassy was the reason for my breakup with Tanner Hughes, my high school boyfriend and first love. Incredibly enough, the two of them were still together. Although their happiness seemed questionable from where I stood, that wasn't any of my business.

"Hey, girls," I said, approaching the table.

Clara's mouth formed a tiny 'o' at the sight of me and Sassy's pleasant expression evaporated.

"What do we do in this situation?" Sassy asked. "Are we supposed to acknowledge the Elephant Man in the room?"

"I had an allergic reaction," I said. I slid into the seat beside Clara. "Something my mother gave me. I'll be fine by tomorrow."

Clara seemed to grasp the situation. As an empath with the Sight, she was familiar with my family's magical chicanery and how I felt about it.

"Did you see Sean?" I asked.

46

"No, where?" Sassy turned around to survey the diner.

"He just left," I said. "He must've ordered something to go."

"Oh, wow," Sassy said. "He must've had a field day when he saw your head."

"I think he might be maturing," I said. "He actually asked if I was okay."

Sassy appeared unconvinced. "Tanner and I saw him at the market on Sunday and he was making fart noises with his armpit."

"Well, he's on duty now," I said, knowing full well that didn't usually make a difference.

"I'm glad you still came to meet us," Clara said. "It's important to keep your chin up."

"She can't," Sassy said, completely serious. "There's too much weight pulling it down right now."

The waitress stopped by to take our order. To her credit, she didn't even blink at the sight of me.

"Are you sure you can eat with those lips?" Sassy asked.

"I'll manage." I looked at Clara. "Working on any good stories?" Clara is a fledgling reporter for *The Buttermilk Bugle*.

"I'm not sure how good it is, but I interviewed Ruben Tasker the other day," Clara said.

"That's funny," I said. "I met his neighbor yesterday, Stuart Riggin. I didn't even realize the Tasker farm was still there until he mentioned it."

"That's the story, in a nutshell," Clara said. "Ruben feels that he's being harassed by certain companies that want to buy his land. He's told them unequivocally no, but they aren't giving up."

"It's understandable," Sassy said. "That farm has been in the Tasker family since the first Puritans settled here."

"What kind of companies are expressing an interest?" I asked.

"Basically, the kind that want to destroy the land," Clara said. "Mary and Ruben have no interest in selling. They're old and I think Ruben's worried the stress is getting to the both of them."

"Why does he want you to write an article about it?" I asked.

"That's easy," Sassy said. "He's hoping if we give the companies bad press, that they'll back off to avoid bad publicity."

"Smart," I said.

"That land is worth a fortune," Clara said. "I'm surprised it's taken this long for companies to take notice."

"I remember my parents had offers during their divorce," I said. Instead of selling, however, the former Wentworth farm had been divided in half as part of the settlement. My father built a new house on 'his' parcel and my mother retained the original farmhouse. The barn straddled the boundary of both properties and was currently being renovated as a small house for me.

"There's one real estate developer that's been driving over there once a week," Clara said. "He started out pleasant enough, but Mary's been getting uncomfortable with his visits."

The waitress approached our table with a tray of food and distributed the plates and drinks.

"Have they spoken to Chief Fox about a restraining order?" I asked.

"In Maryland, it's considered a peace order because it's not a domestic relationship," Clara said. "She'd have to prove that he committed an act that puts her in fear for her safety."

"They shouldn't have to jump through hoops like that just to stop these people from pestering them," Sassy said. "It isn't fair. If someone bothered my grandmother like that, they'd quickly regret it."

I bit back a smile. For someone without supernatural abilities, Sassy was…well, sassy.

"Where did you meet their neighbor?" Clara asked.

"Mr. Riggin was at Coffee with a Cop yesterday. He was talking to Chief Fox about a different issue."

Clara and Sassy exchanged glances. "The one in Magic Beans?" Clara asked.

"Yes," I said.

"Corinne called and asked for a little press on it," Clara said. "Gasper said he'd cover it."

"Really?" I asked. "That's not beneath the star reporter?"

Clara shrugged. "He thinks Corinne is pretty."

"And I suppose you're covering the Tasker farm story because Ruben Tasker is a looker," I joked.

"He's about eighty, but fairly easy on the eyes," Clara said.

"Corinne *is* pretty," Sassy began, "but I still think Chief Fox prefers you. I'm not even sure why he's wasting his time with her when it's clear the two of you have real chemistry."

I stared down at my plate. I couldn't really explain to Sassy why I wasn't dating the chief. She was as clueless as he was when it came to the world of supernaturals.

"It's your family, isn't it?" Sassy asked. "You don't want to subject him to their scrutiny."

"She doesn't want to risk his reputation," Clara jumped in. "Her family isn't the most beloved in town and the chief is still new."

"You're both right," I said. "My family would eviscerate him." Literally. "And it's important that people like and trust him like they did Chief O'Neill. He needs to show he exercises good judgment." And dating a Fury would *not* show good judgment.

"To be fair, that hasn't hurt your sister-in-law," Sassy said. "She married Anton, but she still has a great reputation."

49

"True," I said. "But she heals people. Chief Fox arrests people."

"He keeps the town safe," Sassy said. "It's not so different."

I wish I could explain that Verity's druid powers were designed for healing and mine were designed for...destruction. Not the same at all.

"Well, Eden has made up her mind," Clara said. "I think we should respect that."

Sassy popped a French fry into her mouth. "Let me know if you decide you want to date. I might be able to arrange something for you."

I threw my head back and laughed. "What? A double date with you and Tanner?"

"Well, not with your head in that condition, of course," Sassy said. She scrunched her nose. "Or that outfit."

"Now you sound like my mother," I told her.

Sassy examined me. "It's like you aggressively don't want to attract a man's attention."

"Maybe I don't."

"You're missing out," Sassy said. "I tell Clara the same thing every week."

Clara stole a fry from Sassy's plate. "More like every day."

"Quinn's long gone," Sassy said, referring to Agent Redmond. Clara and the handsome FBM trainer had fallen for each other during his brief stay in Chipping Cheddar, but, unfortunately, the Legolas lookalike had to hit the road.

"Thanks for the reminder," Clara said. She scowled at Sassy over the top of her glass as she drank her iced tea.

"You two are the hottest women in Chipping Cheddar... after me, of course." Sassy paused. "Well, maybe after Amity Dorsey, too, but she's tainted."

"Tainted how?" I asked.

"She had the affair with that minister," Sassy said. "Oh, it was a huge scandal."

"I didn't hear about that," I said.

"They were caught in his Chevrolet right by the big cemetery over near Davenport Park," Sassy said. "He claimed to be helping her get closer to God." She paused. "Amity seemed to be under the misguided belief that calling His name over and over was some kind of direct line to the Man Upstairs. I mean, really. God's not some kind of demon that you summon. That's blasphemy."

I shifted uncomfortably at the mention of demons.

"Amity dated your brother," Clara said. "Don't you remember?"

"Anton dated a lot of girls before he settled on Verity," I said. "I didn't keep a list." I snatched a fry from Sassy's plate and dipped it in Clara's ketchup. "And I don't think you're one to talk about affairs."

Sassy blew a raspberry. "Oh, please. That was high school. Everybody acts stupid in high school. It's all those raging hormones."

"Some raged more than others," I said.

"Besides, I'm still with Tanner, remember?" Sassy said. "And it's not like you want him back." She hesitated. "Do you?"

I barked a short laugh. "Not even if he were the last weasel on earth."

Sassy's eyes locked on me. "Why not even if Tanner were the last man on earth?"

"I said weasel."

"What's wrong with him?" Sassy asked. "He still looks as good as he did in school. Even better, if you ask me. More manly."

I sucked down my iced tea. "If you say so."

Sassy appeared indignant. "Eden Fury, what does that mean?"

I picked at the remainder of my lunch. "It means I don't care. His personality far outweighs his attractiveness."

Sassy bristled. "You're just saying that because of how he treated you."

"It's definitely part of it," I admitted. "I think he's a pathetic jerk who needs a personality transplant. More importantly, I think you, Sassafras Persimmons, can do much better."

Sassy chewed on another fry, seeming to consider my statement. "I love Tanner and I know he loves me."

"Okay," I said. I wasn't about to argue. Sassy was a big girl and had to make up her own mind.

Clara surprised me by saying, "Sometimes love isn't enough."

"Of course it is," Sassy said.

"Love doesn't mean relationship compatibility," Clara said. "If I treated you the way Tanner does, would we still be friends?" She leaned back against the booth. "I think not."

Sassy glanced from Clara to me. "When did this turn into an intervention? I was only trying to help the two of you. No need to turn any tables."

Clara's phone vibrated on the table. "What do you know?" She clicked and brought the phone to her ear. "Hi, Mr. Tasker. Is everything okay?"

Sassy finished the last French fry. "I bet if he was the last man on earth, you'd cave."

"Mr. Tasker?"

She glowered. "You know who I mean."

"You really don't want to let this drop, do you?"

Clara set down the phone. "Mr. Tasker asked me to come back out to the farm."

"Did something happen with the companies that were harassing him?" I asked.

"That's not the reason he asked me to come," Clara said.

"He claims to have discovered a new species of plant and thinks I might want to write an article about it."

"Maybe he'll luck out and discover it's a protected species," I said. "That might help Mr. Tasker shake off the vultures."

"Why don't you come with me?" Clara asked.

"Not me," Sassy said. "I don't even like looking at plants at Home Depot."

Sassy didn't seem to realize that Clara had directed the question to me.

"Should I invite Neville?" I asked. "He's much better at identifying plant life than I would be."

Sassy snorted. "You two work on computers all day. Why would he know anything about rare plant species?"

"Because he's Neville," I said. I shot the wizard a quick text.

"Nerdy by nature," Sassy murmured. "And nerdy about nature."

Clara and I left money on the table. "We'll catch up later," Clara said. She nudged me out of the booth. "You grab Neville and I'll meet you at the farm."

"Sounds like a plan."

Something supernatural was afoot and I couldn't wait to find out what it was.

CHAPTER SIX

I DROVE Neville and I out to the Tasker farm and trudged across a field where Clara awaited us.

"Took you long enough," she said.

I jabbed a thumb in Neville's direction. "Somebody needed the bathroom before we left the office. Too many cups of water today."

"Eight ounces a day," Neville said defensively. "That's the standard. I didn't make the rules."

"Where's Mr. Tasker?" I asked.

"Back at the house," Clara said. "I said we'd come and speak to him after you look at it. The plant is over there. I didn't want to stand too close to it by myself."

"Why?" I asked. I peered over her shoulder in the direction of the plant. "Is it some kind of supernatural Venus flytrap?"

"You tell me," Clara said.

Neville clapped his hands together, practically giddy. "Ooh, I do love botany."

I looked at him askance. "Why does that not surprise me?"

"I had my own greenhouse as a child," Neville said. "I was particularly interested in hybrids."

"That explains your fascination with me," I said.

"Is that like mixing different types of roses and creating a new species?" Clara asked.

"Yes, except I like to mix supernatural species with those native to this world," he replied.

"Neville, you shock me," I said. "That's illegal."

"Why do you think I got recruited for the FBM in the first place?" he asked.

"I assumed it was the magical jewelry you're so good at making," I said. My fingers touched the charmed locket of invisibility around my neck.

"Not at all," Neville said. "My uncle knew about my interests and came to inspect the greenhouse. He had a friend with the FBM, Agent Hertzog. She confiscated the contents of the greenhouse and I didn't speak to Uncle Fred for weeks —that is, until Agent Hertzog contacted me."

"To rub salt in the wound?" I asked.

"No, she was so impressed by my experiments that she offered me a spot upon graduation," Neville said.

"How old were you?" Clara asked.

"I was only thirteen at the time," Neville said.

I whistled. "Wow. I can't imagine what it would have been like to know that I had my dream job waiting for me when I was only thirteen."

"You knew you wanted to work as a federal agent for years," Clara told me. "In fact, I don't remember you expressing an interest in much else."

"That's true," I said. "I was pretty single-minded about it." I broke into a smile. "And yet here I am."

Clara clapped me on the shoulder. "You're still a federal agent, just not in the division you expected."

If I hadn't inadvertently siphoned a vampire's power and

then tried to suck the life out of my old FBI partner, Fergus, I'd still be an FBI agent in San Francisco now. Unfortunately, my supernatural skills didn't involve time travel.

We approached the suspicious plant with caution. If Clara was right and its origin was supernatural, there was no telling what it might be capable of. We had to be careful.

"It's a very bright green, isn't it?" I said.

"And quite complex," Neville added.

"The leaves are segmented," I said. They varied in size and shape as well.

"Technically, they're called fronds." Neville took a step closer to the plant. "Some of the spores are glowing."

It was hard to see the tiny spores with my compromised vision. "What does that mean?"

"I'm not entirely sure," Neville said. "It could be the climate here."

"If only some of the spores are glowing, does that mean it's dying?" Clara asked.

"I'd need to identify the species before I could postulate a theory," Neville replied.

"If it's supernatural, how did it get here in the first place?" I asked. And why was there only one?

"Mr. Tasker said it has to be recent," Clara said. "He walks the perimeter of the farm throughout the week and he came past this spot a week ago. He said it wasn't here then."

"He walks the perimeter every week?" I asked. "That's a lot of walking for an old guy."

Clara smiled. "He said it keeps him healthy and fit. He's also paranoid about adverse possession."

My brow lifted. "The legal concept?"

She nodded. "He thinks if he doesn't walk around the whole farm on a regular basis that someone will be able to claim part of his land."

"And what about Mrs. Tasker?" I asked. "Did she participate?" According to Aunt Thora, the couple that walks together, stays together. She used to point out that my mother always walked ahead of my father and that it was a sure sign they'd eventually split up.

"Apparently, she usually does," Clara said. "Not today, though. He said she didn't seem like herself again, so he left her to do the laundry while he walked. When he found this plant, he called me."

"So I guess he knows enough about plants to know this one doesn't belong," I said, although the glowing spores might have been a hint.

"He even Googled it using reverse image look up," Clara said. "When he didn't find a match, he assumed he'd discovered a new species."

Neville kneeled beside the plant and took a few photos with his phone. "I don't want to disturb it until I know more. Photos will have to do."

"Did Mr. Tasker mention anything unusual at the farm?" I asked. "No issues with animals getting sick, anything like that?"

"No," Clara replied. "His big concern has been the corporate vultures circling. I'm sure if there'd been an issue with any of the animals, he would have mentioned it, if only to blame the companies."

"I think I'll take a few photos and show Aunt Thora," I said. "She's a good resource for supernatural plants. She's convinced that lemon trees are so magical that they had to have originated in Otherworld." I used my phone to take a couple of photos.

"Are you sure we shouldn't just dig it up?" Clara asked.

"I agree with Neville. We need to know more first," I said. "Besides, a dying plant isn't likely to do any harm, supernatural or otherwise. Thanks for looping me in, though."

"It takes a supernatural village," Clara joked.

"What will we tell Mr. Tasker?" Neville asked.

"We have to say something," I said. "I'd rather he not blab about it to other people. The last thing I need is this plant going viral. Once it's online, it's out there."

"Then let's go talk to him now," Clara said. "Mary makes an awesome apple pie. Maybe we'll get lucky and score a slice."

We trudged back to our cars and drove around the fields to the Tasker farmhouse. The white clapboard house was similar to my mother's with a wide front porch and black shutters. A pickup truck was parked in the dirt driveway.

The front door was open so Clara called to him through the screen door.

Ruben Tasker was a slender man, about five foot ten, with a thick head of white hair that looked like clouds. His eyebrows shot up when he saw me beside Clara.

"Hey there, Miss Clara," he said. "I suppose these are the friends you told me about. Didn't mention a genetic condition."

I touched my head, self-conscious. "It's an allergic reaction."

"This is Agent Fury," Clara said. "And her assistant, Mr. Wyman."

I flashed my badge for good measure. To supernaturals and humans with the Sight, it read Federal Bureau of Magic, but to everyone else, it looked like a standard FBI-issued badge.

"You didn't say you were calling the feds," he said. "Is it pot? It's drugs, isn't it? Are you here to arrest me?"

"No, Mr. Tasker. I know you're not responsible for putting that plant on your farm."

He studied me closely. "Your name's Fury?"

"That's right. Eden. I grew up on Munster Close."

He folded his arms. "Beatrice and Stanley's daughter who moved away?"

"Yes, but I came back a few months ago." I suddenly felt like I was an unwitting participant in a staring contest with the farmer.

"And the FBI is interested in my plant?" he asked.

"Yes, sir," Neville interjected. "The botany division."

"There's a botany division?" His tone reflected a healthy level of skepticism. Smart man.

"Of course," I lied. "There's basically a division for everything. If you can dream it, they'll have agents to handle it."

"At my age, nothing surprises me. Come on in." He stepped aside to allow us entry.

"I hope you don't mind that I called Agent Fury," Clara said. "I knew she'd be interested. Plants are her specialty."

I cleared my throat in an effort not to choke. Killing plants was more my specialty.

"Mary, we have more visitors," Mr. Tasker called. "Put the kettle on, would you?"

Clara and I followed Mr. Tasker into the kitchen. It was a pleasant space with floral wallpaper and ceramic chickens on a shelf. The oval wooden table appeared well-worn but otherwise in good condition.

"Clara's back?" Mary Tasker bustled into the kitchen. She was a stout woman with wire-rimmed glasses, white hair, and round, rosy cheeks. If there were an opening for Mrs. Claus at the mall, Mary Tasker would only need to don a red dress.

"Sorry to disturb you again," Clara said. "I called a couple friends to take a look at your plant."

"Oh, yes," Mary said. "That. Ruben is convinced he's made a discovery." She filled the kettle with water and placed it on the stovetop.

"Well, it's not pot, so why is the FBI interested?" Mr.

Tasker sat at the table and gestured for Clara and I to join him.

"I hope chamomile is okay," Mary said. She pulled two mugs from the cabinet.

"Chamomile makes me want to smother myself under the covers and go to sleep," Clara said. "It's perfect."

"Good for me, thanks," I said. I shifted my focus back to Mr. Tasker. "The FBI is interested because it appears to be a foreign species." I neglected to mention just how foreign it might be. "You don't have any idea how it got there?"

The older man shook his head. "Like I told Clara, I do a regular check of my land. It seems to have appeared out of nowhere. Weird-looking thing, isn't it?"

"I'd advise you to steer clear of it, in case it's poisonous," I said.

His eyes rounded. "I should've thought of that myself. Some farmer I am. I was too curious to consider that it might hurt me."

"Did you touch it?" I asked.

"Sure, but I washed my hands when I came in afterward." He stroked his chin. "If it is poisonous and came out of nowhere, do you think it's possible one of them companies is trying to use it to get rid of us?"

"You think one of the companies that's harassing you placed a poisonous plant on your farm to kill you?" I asked. It seemed far-fetched.

"Or make us too sick to put up a fight," Mr. Tasker said. "You'd be surprised what lengths some people will go to for what they want."

No, I really wouldn't.

"What can you tell me about the companies?" I asked.

Mr. Tasker smiled. "You mean you're not going to dismiss me as a conspiracy nut?"

"Not unless you give me a good reason," I said.

He winked at Clara. "I knew I could count on you. You're much smarter than that Cawdrey fella."

"I know," Clara said simply.

I was proud of her for not undervaluing herself like she would've done in high school.

"There's a real estate development company called Brimstone," Mr. Tasker said. "They want the land so they can build a new townhouse community with a lake in the middle. Mr. Brimstone showed me the plans himself."

"A little presumptuous to have plans for land he doesn't own, isn't it?" I asked.

"My thoughts exactly," the farmer said. "He wanted to share his vision, as though it would make me want to hand over the keys to my kingdom."

Beside the stove, Mary wore an amused expression. "*Your* kingdom," she repeated. "I don't think so, dearest."

"You know what I mean."

"And the other company?" I asked.

"Tin Soldiers, Incorporated," Mr. Tasker said. "They want to turn the farm into a junk yard."

I stretched my neck forward. "Seriously? I would think they'd need zoning permission and that isn't likely."

"It is when your company is represented by Jayson Swift," Clara said.

I cringed. Not Jayson Swift. Although the lawyer was human, he could easily pass for one hundred percent slimy demon. It didn't help that he had a seat on the town council.

"What about Brimstone?" I asked.

"He has an in-house team," Clara said.

"Mary isn't particularly fond of Brimstone's head goon," Mr. Tasker said. "What's the man's name again, Mary?"

"Who?" She set a mug in front of each of us and sat beside her husband.

"The one from the real estate developer's office," Mr. Tasker said.

She waved a hand. "Oh, never mind about that. I was being foolish."

Clara's brow knitted. "You told me his visits made you uncomfortable."

"I shouldn't have put it like that," Mary said. "It makes him sound strange."

"Well, maybe he is," I said. "You have a plant of unknown origin on your land. What if it's related?"

"If it's as rare as everyone thinks, then it's likely endangered," Mary said. "A plant like that will likely need to be protected, which means no one could develop the land. We should be doing something to protect it right now. Keep it safe from harm."

"That makes sense," Mr. Tasker agreed. "Who designates plants as endangered? Should I call someone?"

"I'll take care of it, Mr. Tasker," I said. I didn't want attention drawn to the plant with glowing spores. If I wasn't careful, Chipping Cheddar would end up on the internet in connection with alien invasions and I'd be in hot water with FBM headquarters for failing to contain the situation.

"Gus," Mr. Tasker said abruptly.

I looked at him. "Excuse me?"

"Gus is the name of the fella who's been coming around."

Mary didn't react.

"Thanks," I said. "I'll be sure to suggest that he spend his outdoor time in the park instead." And if that 'suggestion' involved a knee to the groin, then so be it.

"Will you need any quotes from me for the article?" Mr. Tasker asked.

Clara shot me a quizzical look.

"I'll have to ask you to keep this under your hat for now,

Mr. Tasker," I said. "Don't mention it to friends or family. It's standard procedure."

He reluctantly agreed.

We said our goodbyes and almost made it back to the car when a familiar sight came into view.

"Stuart?" I said. With dark shadows under his eyes and unkempt white hair, Stuart Riggin looked worse than he had in Magic Beans.

Stuart seemed confused at first, likely because of my swollen head. "Hello again, Agent Fury. Everything okay with your head? It's not a tumor, is it?"

"No, no. Nothing like that," I said. "Just an allergic reaction." To my family. "Neville, Clara. This is Mr. Riggin, the Taskers' neighbor."

"Have you come to examine my wife?" he asked. The hopeful note in his voice pierced my heart.

"Her condition hasn't improved?" I asked.

"Only getting worse," he replied.

"Did you take her for a second opinion like I suggested?" I asked.

Mr. Riggin nodded. "Sure did. I took her to Dr. Verity, just like you said."

"And what did she think?"

"That it could be the early onset of dementia," the old man said. "She wasn't sure at this point. The symptoms weren't conclusive."

"What's the alternative then?" I asked.

"The doctor said to keep an eye on her for now," he said. "She said that Shelley is lucid and her memories are intact." He shrugged. "I tried to explain that all the light's gone out in her eyes. My wife has always had a spark of mischief, if you know what I mean. Not now. Last night, I made a joke about nuns. Shelley loves those kinds of jokes, but she didn't laugh.

Didn't even crack a smile. She just kept on chewing her pork loin."

I felt sorry for Mr. Riggin, but there wasn't much I could do. Medical issues were outside my area of expertise. "Well, I promise you're in good hands with Dr. Verity. I would make sure to follow up with her, especially if your wife's condition starts to deteriorate."

Disappointment rippled across his wrinkled features and I felt a pang of guilt. I desperately wanted to help everyone— that's part of my savior complex, as my mother likes to call it —but even a powerful fury had her limits.

"Shelley's taking a nap, so I thought I'd drop in and chew the fat with Ruben and Mary," he said.

Hopefully, the Taskers would keep quiet about the plant. I didn't need Stuart more anxious than he already was.

"Best of luck, Stuart," I said.

He nodded toward the front door. "Don't need luck. The only thing I need right now is pie."

CHAPTER SEVEN

LATER THAT EVENING, I showed the photos of the plant to Aunt Thora. "Recognize this at all?"

She scrutinized the photos. "Was Princess Buttercup rooting around in Mrs. Paulson's garden again? You'd better be careful or she'll report you to the HOA."

"No, this plant is growing on the Tasker farm. We're pretty sure it's supernatural."

Aunt Thora held the phone closer to her face to examine the photo. "Yes, I can certainly see why you would think that. Such odd spores."

"Can you identify it?" I asked eagerly.

Aunt Thora set the phone back on the counter. "Not without research."

"Oh, are we sharing photos?" My mother swept into the kitchen. "Why don't I show you photos of the Day of Darkness outfits I found? I think they'll look stunning on us."

I groaned. "Mom, I'm working. I don't have time for fashion."

My mother looked me up and down. "You've made that

quite clear." She shoved the phone under my nose. "What do you think of this one? Too much lace?"

"Any lace is too much lace," I said.

She swiped to the next photo. "How about these?" Four women were dressed in black floor-length gowns. One of the dresses had puffy, capped sleeves and another had a plunging neckline. I could guess which one of us the latter dress was for.

"Too formal," I said. "Looks like they're attending a fancy funeral with a full orchestra."

My mother sighed and swiped again. "What about these?"

"Mom, they're all mini-dresses. Grandma won't wear that."

"Neither will I," Aunt Thora said.

"We can make theirs longer versions," my mother said. "That's easy enough." She nudged me. "Come on, Eden. You have my legs. You might as well show them off."

"And here I thought I had my own legs," I replied.

"You should thank me that you didn't inherit your father's legs," my mother said. "They look like plump sausage links."

"I'm not wearing that bizarre hair accessory," I said. It looked like the woman in the photo had black feathers sprouting out of the top of her head. As far as I was concerned, the concealed feathers on my back were quite enough.

"I like that dress," Aunt Thora said, tapping the screen. "Make sure it reaches my ankles though."

"All of Beatrice's dresses reach her ankles," Grandma interjected. "It just depends on which part of the date it is." She looked at me and smiled. "How's your day been? Any passing rabbits mistake your head for a cabbage?"

I glared at her. "The day is almost over, thankfully."

"It was a good day for me," Grandma crowed. "I won my

battles and I collected more Little Critters for the next battle. I'm an unstoppable force."

"I'm sure the local children are thrilled," I said.

Aunt Thora glanced around the house. "Speaking of children, it's awfully quiet here without Ryan and Olivia."

"They were here until after dinner," my mother said. "Just pretend they're asleep in their room."

"That's what you do when they're right next to you," Grandma said.

The remark dredged up flashes of memories—my mother ignoring my stream of chatter while she admired herself in the mirror. My mother forgetting my existence at the clothing store when she became enthralled by the salesman. If she'd been born before Narcissus, the term would now be beatricism.

The James Bond theme song played and I snatched my phone to my ear. I'd switched Neville's ringtone from Harry Potter music when he said he'd rather be associated with Bond's Q than a Hufflepuff. Ouch.

"Hey, Neville."

"I believe I have rather distressing news about our discovery," Neville said.

I walked into the family room for privacy. "It's poisonous?"

"Worse. It's alive."

"Well, duh. Even I know that plants are living creatures. How else can I kill them?"

"You don't understand." Neville cleared his throat, causing the hair on the back of my neck to prickle.

"I need to come to the office, don't I?"

"It would be wise, yes."

"I'll be there as soon as I can."

"Eden, you need to pick a dress," my mother said, as I

hurried past her. My head felt like it was full of jelly when I moved too quickly. I couldn't wait for this hex to lift.

I drove across town to the office as fast as I dared without inviting Deputy Guthrie to pull me over. Holes was closed, but the lights in the tattoo parlor were still ablaze. I noticed the office door was ajar and found Neville hovering near the front of the room. He practically pounced on me when I entered.

"It's a pod demon," the wizard blurted.

"Can you wait until I'm through the door to hit me with bad news?" I closed the door behind me. "What's a pod demon?"

He scurried to his desk and tapped the computer mouse. "This."

I moved behind his chair for a better glimpse of the screen. "How is that a demon?" The image reminded me of dandelion seeds floating through the air.

"It's not a demon," he said.

"Oh, that's a relief."

"It's many demons."

Well, crap.

"Many potential demons," he clarified. He pointed to the wisps of white on the screen. "Those glowing spores we saw on the pod become these."

"And the pod is the plant we found?"

He nodded. "They grow on the pod and disburse when they're ready."

My throat tightened. "Ready for what?"

"Ready to find a host. The spores carry through the air until they either settle inside a host or fail to find one and die."

"And the demon takes over the host?"

"Basically, yes."

I stared at the screen. It was hard to believe those little puffs of cloud could be so dangerous. "What happens to the person when the demon takes over the body?"

"According to the database, the host is slowly drained of its life force."

"So if a demon jumps into a body, the person stays?"

"For a time," he said. "However, you can only share space like that for so long before one of you dies. These demons are designed to kill their hosts slowly."

"At least that means we'll still have a chance to save anyone who's been inhabited." I rubbed my hands over my face, thinking. "We have no idea how many spores are floating around town and who might already be inhabited."

"Not with certainty, no," Neville said. "There's a checklist, though."

"Show me."

Neville opened a new tab. "Top Ten Signs Your Friend Has Been Taken Over By A Pod Demon."

I frowned at him. "Are you sure this isn't from the super-naturallifehacks website?"

"It's official," Neville said.

I started to read the list of signs. "Devoid of emotion. Blank stare. Minimal talking. Sounds like my dad after binge-watching on Netflix." I studied the rest of the list. "Why do they want to take over? Power?"

"They're not trying to take over the world to rule it," Neville said. "Their minds don't work that way. Spreading their seed is in their nature. It's a biological need."

"How do they do it?" I asked. "If spores tried to float up my nose, I think I'd notice." And at least sneeze them out.

"It seems that the spores float in and take over the body while the person sleeps," Neville said.

Got it. "Because the host's resistance is low."

"It's basically nonexistent while they're asleep," Neville said.

I groaned. "So what are our options? Pump Red Bull into the water supply until we've locked down the demon?"

"I doubt that's feasible, Agent Fury."

"Well, come on. You're the invention wizard." I snapped my fingers. "Invent something to prevent everyone from becoming a Stepford demon."

"What do you propose?" Neville asked. "It would be difficult to contain everyone and keep them awake without significant damage. Our options are rather limited."

"How about a reverse Sleeping Beauty spell?" I asked.

He shot me a quizzical look. "I think you've watched one too many princess movies with your niece."

"No, hear me out. You know the part where the fairies put everyone to sleep?" I asked.

Neville fell silent for a moment. "I'm sure I'm supposed to feign ignorance, but how can I? It's a wonderful animated feature." He nodded enthusiastically. "Yes, the fairies use a spell on the kingdom to give Aurora's true love time to find her and wake her with a kiss."

"Right. So what if we do the opposite? A spell that keeps everyone awake until we find a way to get rid of the demon."

Neville settled back in his chair and regarded me skeptically. "How do you propose to keep an entire town of humans awake without explaining to them how it's even possible and, even worse, why it's happening?"

He made a good point. "I don't know yet," I said, "but that seems to be our best line of defense right now."

"It's not a surefire method," Neville said. "As far as we know, sleep just makes it easier for the demon take over. Being awake might slow it down rather than make it impossible." He rubbed his chin. "We also can't discount the impact of sleep deprivation on an entire town. There might be all sorts of accidents as a result. Psychological problems. People border on insanity without sufficient rest."

I felt deflated. "No, you're right. And we can't keep layering spell upon spell to counteract the negative effects."

Neville pondered the information on the screen. "I'll make a few inquiries."

"Do you have a list of supers that you call with questions?"

He swiveled in the chair to look at me. "I'm a member of an online forum. We share information about our experiences that might be helpful to others."

"Like Reddit for wizards?"

"Sort of." His tone was so vague that I couldn't help but dig deeper.

"Is it an official FBM forum?"

"No." He refused to meet my gaze.

"Is it for agents? Should I be on it?"

"There's no need, Agent Fury. You have more than enough to keep you busy."

"I don't know about that. If this forum is helpful, maybe I should be on it."

He fidgeted in the chair. "I don't think you would enjoy it."

"Who cares about enjoying it? We need information and they might have it."

He heaved a sigh. "You can't get it. You...have to be a wizard."

"Well, I have witch in my DNA." I stopped talking when I noticed Neville's hangdog expression. "You mean only wizards, don't you?"

"I'm afraid so."

I gasped. "Sexual discrimination? Neville, how could you?"

"I don't make the rules," he said. "And it's been very informative. The wizards there are top of their game. I don't want to deprive myself of their knowledge, despite their exclusionary tactics."

"No wonder you have a hard time dating," I said. "You spend too much time on single sex forums."

"That might very well be part of it."

I considered him for a moment. "So what's your user name on this forum?"

"Neville123."

"Liar. What's your real user name?"

He hesitated. "GandalfsRevenge917."

I smothered a laugh. "What does the White Wizard have to avenge?"

"Nothing in particular," he said. "I just liked the way it sounds."

"Your birthday is September 17th, isn't it?"

He nodded somberly.

"I'll be sure to mark it on the calendar. I'll buy the donuts that day."

Neville bowed his head slightly. "You're too kind, O' Immortal One."

I smacked his head, careful not to overdo it with my fury strength. "I told you not to call me that."

He rubbed the side of his head. "Forgive me."

"You're forgiven. Can't we just destroy the plant? Dig it up and send it back to Otherworld?"

Neville cut me a disappointed look. "Really, Agent Fury. Did you think it would be that easy? Even if we could, there are likely spores already in circulation."

I hung my head in embarrassment. "I just kind of hoped it would be simple." For once.

"Unfortunately, I haven't found anything definitive on how to stop the spread either," Neville said.

"Are you kidding?" My pulse began to race. We had an invasive demon species in Chipping Cheddar with no clue how to stop it?

"I wish I had better news, Agent Fury. I can assure that I'll continue to research this issue until I find a satisfying resolution."

"I hope these wizards are as knowledgeable as you think," I said. "Text me the second you learn something."

"As you wish."

I left the office, more worried than when I arrived.

I didn't know why I thought it was a good idea to speed home. I knew better. When I saw the red lights flashing in my rearview mirror, I held out hope that it would be the handsome chief behind the wheel.

No such luck.

"Good evening, Deputy Guthrie," I said, injecting a tone of politeness I usually reserved for Shirley, Grandma's God-fearing friend. "Two meetings in one day. What are the odds?"

Sean's pale freckled face appeared outside my window. Something about his vacant expression worried me, especially in light of Neville's discovery. I remembered our recent interaction at the diner—how he failed to insult my swollen head—and I knew. My palms immediately began to sweat on the steering wheel.

"You were speeding," he said. His voice was wooden.

I feigned ignorance. "Was I? Are you sure? I know this is a 40 zone and you know how vigilant I am when it comes to respecting the law."

The deputy barely reacted. "You were speeding. I have to write you a ticket now. License and registration, please."

I flashed a bright smile. "Come on, Sean. Since when do you need to see my license? I'm pretty sure we got ours the same month back in high school, don't you remember? You failed your test the first time."

"I did fail," he said. "My father wasn't happy. He hit me with the belt." He paused. "He always whipped me with the belt when I disappointed him."

I winced at the revelation. "I'm sorry, Sean. I didn't know." Pod demon or not, I couldn't help but sympathize. After all, Sean was human when it happened.

"It's okay," he said. "I'm fine now. I have a great job and lots of responsibility. People respect me. It's a good life."

I dug through my handbag and pulled out my wallet. Unfortunately, the cards had all broken free of their slots—or maybe I just never put them in—and I had to shuffle through them like a deck until I located my license. I handed him the license and then hunted through the glovebox until I found proof of registration.

"Here you go," I said.

Sean studied the license and the slip of paper as though trying to ascertain their authenticity. "You are twenty-six years old."

"Just like you." The longer I sat here, the creepier he seemed—and I already thought Sean was creepy.

"I have so much life left," Sean said. "I'm very fortunate."

"Yes, we both are." No need to tell him about my immortality.

He wrote me a ticket and peeled it off his pad. "It's important to adhere to the speed limit. These limits exist for a reason."

"Yes, sir," I said. Great Goddess, I hated being deferential to this redheaded turd. It was against my nature. "Am I free to go?"

He gave a slight smile. "Have a good evening, Miss Fury."

"Agent Fury," I corrected him. I'd earned that title and he was going to use it.

He tipped an imaginary hat. "Agent Fury."

I waited until he returned to his police car and passed by before pulling back onto the road. I sped toward home and called Neville.

"Sean's a demon," I said, as soon as the wizard answered.

"I didn't think we used demon as a pejorative term in the supernatural community," my assistant said. "It seems rude, given the number of them…"

"No, Neville. I mean an actual pod demon," I said. "The real Sean has been taken over."

He sucked in a breath. "Oh, dearie me. I see. You're certain?"

"One hundred percent. I should have put two and two together already, but I totally forgot about his strange behavior at the diner."

"What happened?"

"He wrote me a speeding ticket."

There was silence on the other end. "That's your proof?" Neville finally asked.

"No. My proof is that he didn't gloat when he gave it to me," I said. "No insults today. No scowl. No emotion. It's like somebody switched off the light upstairs." I stopped talking, remembering Stuart Riggin's description of his wife's behavior. "Oh no. Like Mrs. Riggin."

"Sorry?" Neville said. "Mrs. Riggin turned off lights upstairs? Where?"

I shook my head. "No, no. I think Mrs. Riggin is a pod demon, too. That would explain her sudden change in behavior."

"We have no idea how fast this demon has managed to spread its seed so far," Neville said.

I cringed. "Can you not use expressions like that? It's gross."

"What?" Neville asked. "That's what flowers and plants do. It's how they procreate…"

"I don't need a botany lesson, thanks. We have to figure out how to stop it," I said. If we didn't figure it out soon, we risked losing the entire town to pod demons.

That wasn't a risk I was willing to take.

CHAPTER EIGHT

"I HAVE A PROBLEM," I announced the next morning as I entered the kitchen.

My mother's lips formed a pout. "I know, honey, but all you need is a good pair of tweezers and a few strips of wax and that facial hair will be nothing but a distant memory."

I exhaled loudly. "That's not my problem."

"Well, maybe you don't think so, but I promise you that men have noticed." Her mouth twitched. "At least your head is back to normal. That topical steroid works wonders."

On cue, Ryan pointed to my head and smiled from his high chair.

"I didn't hear Verity drop him off," I said.

"That's because Anton did," my mother said. "You know your brother. He was in stealth mode so he didn't have to talk to us. Practically left Ryan on the front porch with a note."

"Would you like a hot drink?" Aunt Thora offered. "There's tea in the pot and I have fresh wedges right on the counter."

I brushed past my mother and took a ceramic cat mug

from the cabinet. As I poured the tea, Charlemagne appeared at my feet and lifted his head to look at me.

"No begging, Charlemagne," I said. "You know better."

The python continued to stare at me with unblinking eyes.

"This is hot tea and these are lemon wedges," I continued. "Trust me. There's nothing here that you want."

Charlemagne didn't back down. Finally, I relented and tossed the snake a lemon wedge. He gulped it down.

"I swear that Verity left their snake behind because she didn't want to share her meat," my mother complained.

"Yes, because Verity is such a greedy carnivore," I said. "Besides, Charlemagne is like a garbage disposal. He eats anything."

"Charlemagne and your father have something in common," my mother said.

"So what's this problem?" Grandma asked.

I sipped my tea. "There's a new demon in town."

My mother's curiosity was now piqued. "Is he single? Handsome? Doesn't have to be both."

"Definitely not single," I said. "More like multiples. It's a pod demon."

Grandma snapped to attention. "A pod demon, did you say?"

"I did say."

Grandma rose to her feet and shuffled over to us. "Pod demons are no joke. An entire town in Otherworld was wiped out by those suckers."

"And what happened?" I asked. "How did the town keep them from spreading and infecting other towns?"

"They didn't," Grandma said. "The regional council sent in a team."

"A team of what?" I asked.

"The kind of team that makes sure nobody comes out alive," Grandma said ominously.

That was very, very bad news.

"That sounds familiar," my mother said. "Wasn't Stanley involved in that?"

My stomach lurched. "My father was involved?" I wasn't sure why it surprised me. He was a vengeance demon. Who knew how many towns he'd leveled in the name of revenge?

"He wasn't involved in that way," my mother said.

"Go see if your father can tell you more," Grandma said. "All I remember is that he was sent on a job there. By the time he arrived, his target was already eliminated, along with the rest of the town."

"Take your nephew with you," my mother urged. "And that python."

I glanced down at Charlemagne, slithering around the legs of the table in search of crumbs from breakfast. "Why the snake?"

"Because he keeps getting underfoot," my mother complained. "Let that vampire deal with him for an hour or two. Why should I be the only one?"

"You're not the only one," I said. "You don't live alone."

"She thinks she does," Grandma said. "You should hear her sing in the shower."

"If I lived alone," my mother huffed, "there'd be a lot more overnight guests."

"Why? You'd open it as an inn?" Aunt Thora asked.

"More like an in and out," Grandma quipped.

My mother glared at her. "You're just jealous because you haven't had to wear anything except white granny panties since the 1970's."

"Can we get back to the actual problem?" I demanded. "These pod demons are serious."

"You're right, sweetheart," my mother said. She touched

her chin thoughtfully. "Just out of curiosity, do men behave any differently when taken over? For example, say there's a man who hasn't shown any interest in a vibrant, beautiful woman. If he were to be invaded by a pod demon, would he then be inclined to…invade this woman?"

I counted to ten in my head. "If John Maclaren gets taken over by a pod demon, then my barn is never going to get finished." I went to retrieve Ryan from the high chair. "Where's Princess Buttercup?"

"Somewhere in the backyard," Aunt Thora said. "I let her out an hour ago."

"Thanks." I set Ryan on the floor and whistled for Charlemagne. The three of us exited via the back door and walked the five hundred yards to my father's house, where he lived with his second wife, Sally.

I knocked on the kitchen door at the back of the house.

"Pop-pop," Ryan said.

I glanced down at my adorable toothless nephew. "That's right. We're going to see him now."

"Come in," my father's voice called.

I opened the door and Charlemagne forced his way between my feet, nearly knocking me to the floor. Ryan laughed.

"Are you busy?" I asked, as we crossed the threshold into the living room.

My father glanced at the house of cards he'd built on the coffee table. "A little. Why?"

"We came with questions."

"We?" At the sight of Ryan, my father beamed. "Hey! You brought my favorite treat." He ran over and pretended to nibble on Ryan's arm. My nephew screeched with delight.

"Come say hello to me," Sally said. The elegant vampire was busy dusting the mantel of the fireplace. She was the only one I knew who cleaned her house in a dress and pearls.

Ryan shrank away and hid behind my father's shoulder.

"Is your mother making disparaging remarks about Sally again?" my father asked.

"Not that I've heard," I said. I crouched beside Ryan. "Hey, buddy. What's the matter?"

Ryan pointed at Sally. "V'pire."

"That's right," I said. "Sally's a vampire. We already know this."

Sally flashed her fangs and tapped the end of one. Blood bubbled on the pad of her finger. "See? Pointy."

Ryan started to cry. My father hugged him and rubbed his back. "Sally would never hurt you. I can't speak for other vampires, but if one of them ever so much as pinched you, I'd drag them to the bowels of Hell and fling them into the fiery pit myself."

"Dad!" I said sharply.

"What?" my father said. "It's the truth."

"Too graphic."

Ryan's tears subsided and Sally held her arms open. "Come here, sweet child."

Ryan ran to her and flung his arms around her neck. Whatever fear he'd experienced seemed to have dissipated.

"You tell your mother to stop filling that kid's head with nonsense," my father said in an angry whisper.

"Tell her yourself," I said. "I'm your daughter, not an emissary."

Charlemagne slithered over and poked his head up between us like the periscope of a submarine. I stroked his head and his tongue darted out to lick me.

"Did you have to bring the snake?" Sally asked. "He leaves scuff marks all over the floor."

"He wanted to stretch," I said. "He gets bored cooped up in the same place all day."

"That's because he's a python," Sally said. "He doesn't belong as a house pet."

"Tell that to everyone else," I said. I wasn't in the mood to field their complaints against the other side of my family. I had more important business to attend to.

"I saw on the calendar that the Day of Darkness is coming up," my father said.

"You remember?"

"Of course I remember," he said. "I had to buy those black streamers every year. Do you know how hard it is to buy black streamers unless it's October?"

"The internet makes it easy now," Sally said.

"Where was the internet when I was first married?" my father demanded. "I used to go to this little shop in Otherworld called Back in Black. It was owned by a dwarf called Milliken. Everything he sold was black. And I mean everything."

Sally brightened. "Oh, I know that place. I bought a cloak there. It billowed so much at the bottom that I felt like a queen in a gown."

My father kissed her cheek. "A queen should be so lucky." His phone buzzed in his back pocket and he fumbled to retrieve it.

"Is that Myrtle again?" Sally asked. "Tell her you're not doing any more blood donations until she returns my hoop earrings."

His face lit up as he read the screen. "Good news. The Baskin job is on."

Sally glanced up at him. "Really? I thought it was going to be too difficult because the father and son live so far apart."

"Family reunion in Otherworld." My father punched the air. "It's a twofer." He cut a glance in my direction. "Long-standing vendetta between the Baskins…"

"Let me guess—and the Robbins?" I asked.

"Very funny, but no," my father said. "The Swarovski family. Johann Swarovski hired me to…"

I held my hands over my ears and sang loudly, drawing Ryan's attention. He placed his small hands over his ears and copied me. Pretty soon all four of us stood there with our hands covering our ears and singing at the top of our lungs. Ryan's laughter soon overtook his singing. He collapsed on the floor, delirious with glee.

"Oh, to be a toddler again," I said. Before I knew that my father was a diehard vengeance demon and that, even worse, he took great pride in his work.

"And have no independence?" Sally asked. "Your nephew can barely walk without assistance."

"Like your mother after too many cocktails," my father said. "Come to think of it, she drools and babbles too."

I glared at him. "What have I told you about making negative comments about Mom in front of me or your grandchildren?"

My father paused. "Make them funnier?"

I groaned. "Just stop. I don't need the stress. I have enough to contend with right now."

"Is it your mustache?" Sally asked. "I was going to mention it, but didn't want to upset you."

My fingers instinctively touched the area above my upper lip. "What mustache?"

Sally quickly looked away. "Never mind. I was hallucinating. Must be that new herbal tea." My mother and Sally had more in common than they liked to believe.

"There's a situation in town," I said. "That's actually the reason I'm here."

My father rolled his eyes. "I should've known better than to think you'd come purely for the joy of spending time with your family. Would it kill you to make more time for us?"

"It might," I said.

"So what's this situation?" my father asked. "More supernatural trouble?"

"I bet it's the werewolves," Sally said. "Not Julie and Meg, of course, they're lovely. Probably the Phelps family again. I bet one of them shifted and was spotted by humans on a camping trip. Am I right?"

I stared at her blankly. "Where are you getting this?"

Sally returned her attention to Ryan. "They're primeval, that family."

"They're not," my father objected. "They're so low on the evil scale that they barely register."

I smacked my forehead. "That's not what primeval means, Dad."

"Naturally, Aunt Eden knows what it means," my father said to Ryan in a toddler voice. "How else can she pass judgment if she doesn't know all the words?"

I heaved a sigh. Why I thought my father would be a good resource was beyond my comprehension?

"I found a plant at the Tasker farm," I said.

My father craned his neck to look at me. "Congratulations?"

"It's not an ordinary plant. It's a pod with glowing spores."

"Sounds beautiful," Sally said. "Maybe I could plant some in the garden. Mrs. Paulson would be green with envy."

"You don't want this plant in your yard," I said. "Turns out it's a pod demon."

My father's mouth dropped open. He shifted to his bottom on the floor next to Ryan as beads of sweat pilled on his forehead.

"Stan?" Sally asked, her alarm evident.

My father kept his focus on me. "You're sure?"

I nodded. "Neville and I are researching next steps, but Grandma mentioned that you've encountered them before. I thought you might have insight."

"Not directly, thank the devil," he said, and repeated the story Grandma told me. "It was one of the worst atrocities I've ever seen, and that's saying something."

"You weren't around for the Vampire Revolution in Otherworld," Sally said. "Talk about atrocities. That's when many vampires escaped to this world, to avoid persecution."

"That's genuinely interesting," I said. I was a sucker for history, no pun intended. "But right now I have to concentrate on pod demons. Is there another way to stop the species from invading without killing all the hosts?"

"If there is, I haven't heard it," my father said.

I thought of the people I suspected were already infected. Although there was no love lost between Sean and me, that didn't mean I wanted him dead. And poor Mrs. Riggin. Her husband thought she was suffering from dementia.

"In my experience, the policy has been to eviscerate everything connected to the pod demon to prevent it from spreading," my father said. "It's the scorched earth approach. Deadly but effective."

"We can't let that happen to Chipping Cheddar," Sally said. "This is our home." She hugged Ryan close to her and he babbled incoherently. My mother could complain about Sally's coldness all she liked, but the grandchildren clearly adored her.

"The spores tend to infiltrate while we're sleeping. We should stay awake as much as possible," I said. "Make it harder for the spores to invade."

"That's easy for me," Sally said. "Vampires don't need sleep. It's merely a habit we developed to fit into society."

"Then you need to help my dad," I said.

"I need a solid eight hours of sleep or I'm a nightmare," my father said.

I remembered. As kids, if we disturbed my father's sleep,

Anton and I would be forced to wear an oversized T-shirt for the rest of the day.

The same T-shirt.

At the same time.

Needless to say, sharing clothing with my big brother who constantly tormented me while flexing his vengeance demon muscles was not an enjoyable experience.

"I can watch over him when he sleeps," Sally said. "If I see any spores coming his way, I'll destroy them."

"Dee-troy," Ryan repeated.

My father clapped. "That's right, Ryan. Destroy." He tickled the little boy's stomach. "You are going to be a fierce one, aren't you?"

Ryan laughed and clutched his stomach.

"I don't remember you tickling me like that," I said.

"I didn't have to," my father said. "You had your own hand to do it."

"That severed hand that you brought back from Otherworld on a business trip?" I shuddered at the memory. "No thank you." I hated that hand. It reminded me of Thing from The Addams Family.

"You were always so ungrateful," my father said.

"A thimble with the name of the town would have been preferable," I said.

My father poked Ryan gently in the soft flesh of his tummy. "How about you, little demon spawn? Would you like a nice severed hand from Otherworld?"

"Verity would kill you," I said.

"He could keep it here and play with it when he visits," my father said.

Sally seemed uncertain about this arrangement. "Does it bleed? You know how difficult it is to remove bloodstains and I'm an expert."

"It doesn't bleed," my father said. "In fact, it might be

useful. It could do the dusting." He gestured to her feather duster on the mantel.

Sally perked up. "In that case, I'll consider it."

I bounced a ball on the floor and both Ryan and Charlemagne went after it. "So you have no more ideas about the pod demon? No useful advice to offer?"

My father gave it another thought and said, "Try not to die this week or next. I'll be out of town and I can't reschedule."

"That's..." I shook my head. "I'll do my best."

CHAPTER NINE

I LEFT Ryan and Charlemagne at my father's and drove into town. The more I thought about the pod demon takeover, the more frightened I became. I had to learn more about the pod. How had it gotten on the Tasker farm? Was it simply drawn to the area the way other supernaturals are—because of the energy from the dormant portal? Or was there a more nefarious purpose? I needed to check out the two companies interested in acquiring the land. If one of them had supernatural ties, it was possible they were involved.

I glanced at the passenger seat where the speeding ticket still rested from yesterday. I'd have to pay it…or maybe this was a good excuse to check on Chief Fox. What if he'd been taken over like Deputy Guthrie? I'd never forgive myself if anything happened to him.

I decided to swing by the chief's office before I followed up on the Tasker companies. I parked on the street, not far from the station. As I rounded the corner of the block, I came face-to-face with Tanner Hughes. Inwardly, I groaned. Now wasn't the best time for a run-in with my ex.

"Hey, Tanner," I said.

"Good morning, Eden."

I brushed past him and was shocked when he didn't try to grab my wrist or make an insufferable innuendo. I stopped in my tracks and turned to face him. "You look nice today."

"Thank you," he said. "You look lovely as well. I like your hair that length. Then again, I've always preferred long hair."

"Good thing Sassy has long hair," I said.

"I'd love her just the same if she were bald," Tanner said.

Well, that settled it. Another pod demon. Tanner Hughes seemed to have had a much-needed personality transplant, courtesy of a supernatural invasion.

"You're sweet to say that," I said. "You used to say sweet things like that to me." Not really, but I had to be sure.

"Life is simpler when people get along," Tanner said. "Kindness costs us nothing."

"So true," I said. Poor Sassy. Knowing her, she wasn't going to like this new version of Tanner one bit.

"Have a wonderful day," he said, and I wanted to hurl.

I continued to the police station and stopped at Judith's desk. "Is the chief in?"

The old woman peered at me. "Are you selling something? Because there's no solicitation here."

"No, Judith. It's me. Agent Fury." I showed her my badge.

"Oh, right. Go ahead in."

"Thank you." I continued past her desk to the chief's door and poked my head through the doorway. "Hey there. Got a minute?"

"For you?" He broke into a broad grin. "I have at least two."

"Ha, very funny." I entered the office and closed the door behind me.

He motioned to my head. "Looks like your noggin's back to normal. Maybe some damage on the inside?"

"Inside's functioning normally," I said.

The chief wore a hint of a smile. "You didn't look so bad with that giant head."

I gave him a menacing look. "Liar."

"I'm thinking you should use that shampoo again on Halloween," he teased.

I was relieved to hear him joke with me, even if the joke was at my expense. Based on my limited information, I got the impression that pod demons didn't have a sense of humor.

"Deputy Guthrie gave me a speeding ticket yesterday," I said.

He chuckled. "Ah, so that's why you're here."

I retrieved the ticket from my handbag and dangled it in front of him. "I contest."

He plucked the ticket from my fingers. "You know you have to contest it in court and not to me, right?"

"When's the next Coffee with a Cop?" I asked. "I'll make sure to stop by with my list of grievances."

His sea-green eyes twinkled. "Now there's a list?"

I maintained a neutral expression. "There's always a list."

"I hope you're not catching whatever's gotten into Corinne," the chief said. "She was so odd last night."

I froze. "Last night?" I didn't want to imagine what the twosome got up to in the wee hours.

"We went out for dinner and she barely said a word," he continued. "She's usually pretty good company, so I asked if anything was wrong. She said no."

"And you believed her?"

He shrugged. "I don't know what to think. She didn't seem angry or anything. Just sort of blah."

Anxiety coiled in my stomach. "Would you say that maybe the light went out in her eyes?"

A grin tugged at his lips. "Well, she doesn't shine like

some supernovas I've met in this town, but yeah, I guess you could say there was a certain dullness about her."

"Everyone has off days," I said vaguely. How could I explain to the chief that his date had been overtaken by a pod demon?

"I'm sure you're right. I'm probably overthinking it."

"Do me a favor, Chief," I said. "Keep your windows closed at night."

"This time of year?" he said. "The weather's perfect in the evenings. I love a light breeze when I'm in bed. Alone," he added hastily.

"It's the pollen," I lied. "Verity says it's terrible right now and that even people with no history of allergies are going to suffer."

"And you don't want to see me suffer?" He grinned. "That's sweet of you." He ripped my speeding ticket in half. "I'll take care of this for you. Can't have our federal agents taking time away from their work to show up in traffic court, can we?"

"Thanks, Chief. You're the best." I spun on my heel and practically skipped out of the office. Chief Fox had that effect on me. My body wanted to either float or skip or turn to jelly whenever he was within reach.

On my way back to the car, a call from Neville came through. "I'll be there shortly," I said. "I'm making a couple of stops first."

"Good. I have an update for you, Agent Fury, and you're not going to like it."

My whole body tensed as I slipped behind the wheel. "Definitely not when you open with a statement like that. What is it?"

"I wasn't getting anywhere on the wizard forum, so I decided to make a few inquiries at FBM headquarters," he said.

My fingers gripped the phone. "And?"

"And if we hope to live through this, we need to keep the situation between us."

Between us? "Why? What did they say?"

"According to my source, the FBM's response to pod demons is swift and immediate," Neville said. "They will destroy the entire town and everyone in it."

My pulse raced. "But how? How could they get away with it in this world?"

"By labeling it as an unfortunate gas explosion would be my guess," Neville said. "Report that the fire spread quickly and firefighters were unable to contain it."

My gut twisted, Bavarian pretzel-style. "We have to make sure the FBM doesn't get wind of this. Didn't they wonder why you were so interested?"

"I told them I'm writing a screenplay about an alien invasion. I had multiple offers of help after I said that."

I relaxed slightly. "You're a genius," I said.

"A real genius would be able to take care of the pod demon without risking thousands of lives," Neville said.

"Don't be too hard on yourself, Neville. We'll figure this out together."

"I have every confidence in you, Most Exalted One."

I was glad Neville had confidence in me because, right now, he was the only one.

The office for Tin Soldiers was a little tricky to find, but I managed. Funnily enough, it was located on the same street as the FBM office, albeit closer to the train tracks. The reception area was practically nonexistent with an unmanned metal desk with a matching chair, and a single chair for visitors pushed against the wall. The decor was tin chic with a variety of designs all made from painted metal. There were sunflower heads, cat sculptures, and a variety of wire silhouettes. I was admiring a rainbow-colored metal heart when a middle-aged man limped into the room. His hair was brown and thinned to a mere layer of wisp. He wore a T-shirt with the logo for the band AC/DC and baggy jeans.

"I thought I heard the door. Can I help you?" he asked. "The dollar store is two doors down."

"I'm Agent Fury." I showed him my badge and his brows drew together.

"You're from the…?"

"That's right. FBI."

"I see." He smoothed the thin layer on the top of his head. "I'm Bruce Fendall, president of Tin Soldiers. What brings you to my doorstep, Agent Fury? Is your office looking for some new designs? We have quite a collection, I can assure you."

"No designs today, Mr. Fendall. I have questions about your interest in the Tasker farm."

His expression changed to one of enlightenment. "Mr. Tasker complained about my inquiries, I take it."

"I think he used the word harassment rather than inquiry," I said.

"Oomph." He pretended to clutch his stomach. "I consider myself a professional."

"A professional stalker?"

The muscle in his cheek twitched. "A connoisseur of scrap metal."

"That sounds highly specific."

"Oh, it is and I take my business very seriously."

"So you want to turn the Tasker farm into a junk yard," I said.

"There are few spaces in Chipping Cheddar with the land for such an endeavor," Bruce said. "The Tasker property is ideal for what I have in mind."

"And what happens? People dump their scraps there and you polish turds into diamonds?"

"More or less," he said. He smiled, revealing a set of slightly crooked teeth. No orthodontia for this guy. Although my father had been against nonessential procedures, my mother had been adamant that we wore braces if we needed them and threatened my father with a hex on his nether regions if he got in the way. Needless to say, Anton and I sported matching camera-ready smiles.

"Can't you rent a storage unit for that?" I asked. "Do you really need a whole farm? That's a lot of acreage for junk."

"Your trash is our treasure," he said. "It's our company slogan."

"Nice." I was perfectly willing to acknowledge a good slogan when I heard one.

"I'm trying to grow my business," Bruce said. "For that, I need adequate space. The Tasker farm would provide it and then some."

"Do you work alone?" I asked.

"For the most part. I outsource as much as I can," he said. "It keeps costs down."

"The farm's worth a lot of money," I said. "Are you sure you can even afford it?"

Bruce smirked. "If the FBI is interested in my profit and loss statements, I'm sure they can find a way to access them."

"I understand Jayson Swift represents your company."

"That is correct," Bruce said. "I find Jayson to be worth every penny the company pays him."

And I found Jayson to be a skeezeball, but why argue?

"If you need further information, feel free to contact him," Bruce continued, "though I'm happy to answer any more questions you may have."

Bruce Fendall may have had an unusual business, but he seemed more like an annoying guy than a harassing mobster-type figure. And as a regular human, he wouldn't know anything about a plant from Otherworld or pod demons.

"Do you know anything about the other company that's been sniffing around the farm?"

Bruce's expression soured. "Brimstone."

"You know the company?"

"The man and the company, unfortunately," Bruce said. "Not that we run in the same circles, mind you. Titian Brimstone wouldn't give a guy like me the time of day."

"Then how do you know him?"

"We've been going after the same types of properties recently," he said. "Different plans for them, of course, but similar requirements."

"What do you think of him?"

Bruce removed his hands from his pockets and hooked his thumbs through the belt loops. "Arrogant. Pompous. Single-minded. Ruthless."

Ruthless.

"Wow, such praise. Sounds like you have a bit of a crush," I said.

Bruce snickered. "Brimstone belongs in a metropolis somewhere, not here in Chipping Cheddar. Leave a place like this to the little folks."

"So they can turn trash into treasure?"

He winked. "Exactly."

"I don't have any more questions at the moment," I said. "Just a request. Leave the Taskers alone. They've told you unequivocally no. They're old and vulnerable and they don't need strangers creeping around their property. It's unsettling."

He slid his hands into the pockets of his jeans. "Very well then. They'll not hear another word from me unless I hear from them first."

"You spit and swear on your mother's grave?"

He peered at me. "Is that how the FBI conducts business now?"

No, that's how the Fury family conducts business. "Not really. I'm trying to keep this visit off the books so you're not on our radar. I imagine you'd prefer to avoid a tax audit."

"Cunning, Agent Fury. A subtle threat." He gestured to the metal sunflower on the wall. "Any interest? I'll cut you a deal."

"Bribery, Mr. Fendall? Cunning. I don't think a sunflower would do the trick, but thanks. I have a sun lamp in my office and that's basically all I need."

"A sun lamp?"

"It was a special gift," I said. "There's not a lot of natural light in my office."

"Yes, mine is similar, as you can see."

A train rumbled past and the walls shook. "We don't have that," I said.

"I like trains," he said. "Always have."

"A train's just a chain of metal boxcars, right? What's not to love?"

"You understand me already," Bruce said. "Such a rare gift, to be understood."

"Even rarer to be understood and accepted," I said. I knew that all too well.

"Tell me, Agent Fury, will you be delivering the same message to Brimstone that you delivered to me?"

I frowned. "Of course. I don't play favorites, Mr. Fendall, no matter how much money and power someone appears to have. They all get treated the same."

Bruce observed me for a long beat. "Yes, the same," he said. "Please be sure to give my regards to the Taskers."

I wagged a finger. "Remember the rules, Mr. Fendall. Only if they give their regards first." He escorted me to the door and I came to an abrupt stop.

"Be sure to sleep with your windows closed," I said.

He seemed taken aback. "Another threat, Agent Fury?"

I quickly realized how my suggestion might have sounded. "No, no. This allergy season is brutal with the pollen count and my doctor is advising everyone to seal up any gaps and keep windows closed."

"I appreciate the warning," he said. "I haven't felt like myself this past week."

Oh, he had no idea how much worse it could be. If he ended up like Tanner, Sean, or Shelley Riggin, he could cease to be himself at all.

CHAPTER TEN

STANDING OUTSIDE THE BRIMSTONE BUILDING, I got the sense that Bruce Fendall wasn't wrong about Titian Brimstone. The building towered over its corporate neighbors and the ostentatious canopy over the entrance boasted financial abundance.

I crossed the black and white marble floor of the lobby and approached the reception desk. The woman behind the desk looked like she spent too much time on a boat without sunscreen. Not uncommon for some residents. She greeted me with a toothy smile.

"Welcome to Brimstone," she chirped. "I'm Carly. How can we be of service today?"

"I'd like to see Mr. Brimstone," I said.

"Do you have an appointment?" Her tone suggested that she knew very well I didn't.

I whipped out my badge. "Nope, but tell him I've got a box of his favorite Girl Scout cookies and I'm sure he'd be interested in talking to me."

Carly's brow furrowed. "The FBI sells Girl Scout cookies now?"

"No. That was just a quip," I said. I shoved my badge in my pocket. "One of those cool things you say to introduce yourself."

Carly cocked her head. "If you say so."

"Please tell Mr. Brimstone that a federal agent wishes to speak with him," I said.

"I'll see if he's available, Agent Fury. One moment, please." She turned away to buzz her boss.

I took a moment to survey the interior of the building. The soothing gray walls were adorned with oversized artwork of abstract nature scenes. I had no doubt they'd been commissioned especially for this building. The sizes and colors were too perfect for the space to have been mass-produced.

"Mr. Brimstone will see you now," she said. "Take the elevator to the top floor."

"Thank you." My flats padded across the marble floor and I heard the echoing click of someone's high heels behind me.

A statuesque woman joined me in the elevator and hit the button for the top floor before I could reach it. "I'll escort you," she said. "I'm heading there myself." She stuck out a hand. "Katy Brimstone, Titian's wife."

I shook her hand. "Agent Eden Fury."

I caught her look of surprise. "An agent? Is there an EPA issue again?"

"Not EPA," I said. "I'd rather save the particulars for your husband, Mrs. Brimstone."

She hesitated. "Should I not be present for this meeting?"

"That's up to your husband."

"I'm an officer of the company," she said. "If there's a problem, I should probably be aware."

I gave her a reassuring smile. "I don't know that there is a problem. I'm here to discuss your husband's interest in a local farm."

"Tasker," she said, more of a statement than a question.

I said nothing as the elevator doors opened and dumped us directly into Mr. Brimstone's office. He stood at the window, tall and muscular with a torso like a tree trunk. He turned at the sound of his wife's footsteps and I was struck by the squareness of his jaw. The shape was so severe that it was almost comical.

"Katy, I didn't realize you were back." They met in the middle of the room and he offered his wife a peck on the cheek.

"I brought a friend." She nodded to me. "This is Agent Eden Fury."

I showed him my badge. I wasn't sure about Katy, but I knew immediately that Titian Brimstone was a demon. Supernaturals weren't always that easy to identify, but his aura screamed demon.

"My receptionist doesn't have the Sight," he said. "She told me you were FBI, not FBM."

"I figured," I said.

Katy glanced from her husband to me. "FBM?"

"Federal Bureau of Magic, my lamb," Mr. Brimstone said.

"I didn't realize such a thing existed," his wife said.

"Katy's human," he explained, sounding almost apologetic. "But she's a fast learner."

"I get an undeniable demon vibe from you," I said.

Mr. Brimstone's laugh boomed. It was the kind of laugh that came straight from his massive chest and exploded into the world.

"A business in the streets and a demon in the sheets," his wife said.

Mr. Brimstone winked at her. "That's an understatement." *Sheesh. Get a room.*

"What kind of demon, may I ask?"

"A hellion," he said. "I immigrated here decades ago.

Started a new life." He smiled. "Met Katy five years ago and haven't looked at another woman since then." They exchanged an affectionate look and I couldn't decide if he was genuine or placating his wife.

"So you bring the brimstone," I said.

His expression darkened. "I bring the fire, too, should the need arise."

"Did you tell the Taskers that when you paid them a visit?" I asked.

He leaned his bottom against the edge of his desk. "Is that what this is about? My interest in purchasing the farm?"

"The Taskers feel that they're being harassed," I said. "Mrs. Tasker said that you've sent someone around every week."

"It's not unusual when you're trying to develop a business relationship," he said.

I wasn't buying it. "She's an old woman, Mr. Brimstone. It isn't right."

Mr. Brimstone eyed me curiously. "And what interest does the FBM have in an elderly human couple?"

"It's part of our job to keep supernaturals from scaring humans," I said.

"I'm running a business," he objected. "The fact that I'm a supernatural and they're not is neither here nor there."

"I disagree. There's an imbalance of power and you know it."

He regarded me silently for a moment. "As I understand it, your family lives on one of the original Chipping Cheddar farms, Agent Fury," he said.

An uneasy chill traveled up my spine. Why did he know anything about my family? "That's right. The Wentworths were the original owners." And Alice lived there still, not that he needed to know that. I was the only one who could see Alice, thanks to my fury powers.

"And how did they obtain such a coveted piece of property?" he asked.

"They paid for it in the usual way," I said. "The farm went up for sale and their offer was accepted."

He took a step toward me. "Is that so? They didn't intimidate anyone with their black magic or threats of vengeance?"

It seemed that somebody was keeping close tabs on the other supernaturals in town.

"Why would they?" I replied. "The Wentworths didn't know what they were. The last members of the family decided to sell."

"That's what you've been told. Make no mistake, your family isn't known for its soft touch."

I bristled. "Let me put it this way, Mr. Brimstone. Even if my family did unfairly obtain the farm—and I'm not conceding that they did—that doesn't mean I'll let you do the same."

"Special treatment, eh? And here I'd heard you were unfailingly *good*." He snorted. "I should have known better. No one could live in such a dark shadow and not succumb eventually."

Katy shifted from one heel to the other, visibly uncomfortable. "If you don't need me, I think I'll go check in with Martha in accounting."

Brimstone blew her a kiss. "Go on, lamb. We'll catch up later."

Katy hurried from the room so fast that I worried she'd break a heel on the way out.

"I am nothing like my family," I said, trying not to seethe.

Brimstone laughed again, more softly this time. "Sounds like I hit a raw nerve."

Now it was my turn to hit a raw nerve. "Have you ever used the services of a demon to acquire a property that you wanted?" I watched him closely for a reaction. "Maybe import something from Otherworld in an effort to *persuade* them?"

His expression hardened. "That's racist. Just because I'm a demon doesn't mean I'd stoop to such levels. I run a solid business here."

I kept pushing. "If you were going to employ the services of a demon, which kind would be your go-to?"

"Depends on the services," he said. "I mean, I know your father and brother would be good for a revenge project. You've got that lawyer cousin, too."

"Uncle," I corrected him. Uncle Moyer. "That's not the kind of services I mean."

His brow furrowed. "I don't retain those type of services anymore. Maybe in my younger days before I embarked on actual relationships. I definitely dated my fair share of demons. To be honest, I never imagined I'd end up with a human partner. Hellions and humans aren't exactly a common combination."

"Neither are furies and humans," I said. My thoughts automatically turned to Chief Fox. "Out of curiosity, did you tell Katy before you married her?"

"About my origin?"

I nodded. "It can't be easy for a human to accept."

"I eased her in," he said. "Dropped hints every so often."

"How do you drop a hint like that?" It was more like a nuclear bombshell.

"You've never dated a human? A pretty woman like you?" He looked me over. "I find that hard to believe."

"I dated a moron," I said. Tanner never had a clue. Still didn't. I felt a slight pang of guilt remembering that his body now housed a pod demon. What if Tanner was gone for good?

"Only one?" Brimstone asked. "You got off easy."

I laughed, despite the tension. "I find it best to keep them at bay."

"I had Katy watch certain films and TV shows and then gauged her reaction to them. She liked all the vampire movies. Had the hots for the males." He shrugged. "Tall, dark and brooding. I figured I was on the right track."

"How did you decide it was safe to reveal your true self?"

"We watched Hellboy. Do you know that comic? They made a movie or two."

I nodded. "And what? She didn't shudder with fear?"

"No. In fact, she added Hellboy to her laminated list."

"What's that?" I asked.

"Of people she's allowed to sleep with should the opportunity ever present itself."

"I guess that made it clear for you."

"Made the risk worth taking. Paid off, too, as you can see."

I could. Regardless of his questionable business practices, he seemed to be in a healthy relationship with a human. Hats off to him for that.

He edged closer to me. "Tell me, Agent Fury. What's your interest in my personal relationship?"

"Any time a demon and a human interact, I'm interested," I said. "It's my job."

"The government has no place in our private lives."

"I'm not issuing any mandates, Mr. Brimstone. I was only making conversation."

"I'm a busy demon, Agent Fury. Any more questions or are you just stalling to spend more quality time with me?"

"Oh, stop," I said. "You're obviously very much in love with your wife. Don't use flirtation as a weapon. It just makes you look like a jerk."

His arms dropped to his sides. "You weren't even a little tempted?"

"Not really, sorry. Maybe if I hadn't seen you two together." I didn't believe he'd cheat on his wife with me. I did, however, believe he'd kill me if it suited him. I decided to keep that nugget to myself. Best not to give the hellion any ideas.

"Poor timing then," he said.

"Do you know Handel Gottsberg?" I asked.

He didn't flinch. "Yes. We do occasional business together."

"Any recent business?"

"No. He was in town and offered to meet—see whether I needed anything—but my schedule was already booked for his timeframe."

"So you didn't see him?"

"No, you can check with Katy, if you like. She keeps my calendar."

"One more question," I said. "Do you know anything about a supernatural plant growing on the property?"

"Really? How interesting."

"More worrying than interesting. It's spawning pod demons."

Deep lines appeared across his wide brow. "Are you telling me there are pod demons in Chipping Cheddar?"

"You know what they are?"

"Unfortunately, yes." He shivered. The large hellion actually shivered. Now I knew we were in trouble.

"Somehow a plant rooted itself on the Tasker farm and released spores, spawning pod demons. I was wondering if you had anything to do with that."

"Do I look insane to you? Do you know what happens with pod demons?"

"I've had to learn pretty quickly," I said. "So you had nothing to do with putting that on their farm in order to get them to sell?" I had to be careful now. If Brimstone had nothing to do with the pod demon, I didn't want word to get back to the FBM that we had a situation.

"By the devil, no. I don't want to be taken over by one of those nasty suckers," he said. "They're disgusting, not to mention dangerous."

I wasn't sure whether to believe him, but something in his expression suggested his response was genuine. "I need you to keep this to yourself for now. If my headquarters gets wind of this, they won't hesitate to destroy the town and everyone in it." If anything, that would appeal to his sense of self-preservation.

"The whole town? What about my buildings?"

"They favor gas leak explosions," I said. "More believable in this world."

Brimstone rubbed the top of his head. "This changes things."

"You don't want the farm anymore?" A silver lining, at least.

"I didn't say that." He paused, thinking. "Let me know if you manage to get rid of them."

"Trust me," I said. "You'll know if I don't."

I strode out of his office and back into the elevator. On the way down, the elevator stopped on the third floor and a man and a woman got on. They were both in tailored suits and shiny shoes. They were in the midst of a conversation.

"Do you really think so?" the man asked.

"You're ridiculous, Gus," the woman said. She threw her head back and gave a throaty laugh.

I swiveled to face him. "You're Gus?"

He met my inquisitive gaze. "Yes. Have we met?"

"No, my name is Agent Fury," I said. "It's my understanding that you've been spending time over at the Tasker farm uninvited. Is that true?" Despite her retraction, I could understand why Mary Tasker initially felt uncomfortable with visits from Brimstone's henchman.

His thin lips compressed further, a sure sign of stress—and possible guilt. "It's a lovely property."

"And the Taskers are lovely people. They don't deserve to be harassed."

"I think I've been doing them a favor. They get lonely on that big farm all by themselves."

I didn't care for Gus whatsoever. "Maybe you should give your visits a rest."

"Is that a threat?" he asked, smirking. "Hard to take it seriously from a girl who isn't even packing heat. What kind of agent are you anyway?"

"The kind that doesn't need a gun to get what she wants." The elevator doors opened and I flashed a bright smile before stepping out. "Have a nice day."

CHAPTER ELEVEN

I ARRIVED home to find the house unnaturally calm. Usually late afternoons meant a house bursting with noise and activity because Olivia and Ryan were here wreaking havoc until one of their parents came to collect them.

Right now was eerily quiet.

A low growl brought me to the bedroom door of the guest room. The door was closed and Princess Buttercup lay in the hallway in front of it, giving the threshold her undivided attention.

"What's the problem?" I asked, stroking her head. "Are they excluding you again?" Charlemagne and Olivia were thick as thieves and sometimes their playtime resulted in the hellhound and the cat feeling left out. Well, maybe not the cat. Candy generally preferred her isolation.

I clicked open the door to see Olivia passed out on the bed with Charlemagne tucked under arm. How a Burmese python could curl up into such a tight ball on a single bed, I had no idea, but there he was. It seemed playtime had worn them both out.

I stood beside the bed for a moment, observing my niece's

serene expression. What was it like to be so innocent and unburdened? If I'd ever felt that way, I couldn't remember it now. I wanted Olivia to have a normal childhood, one without the pressure of developing her powers or erring on the side of evil. I knew Verity was a good mother and would be a full supporter of Team Good, but whether the druid and I would be enough of an influence to keep Olivia and Ryan from the dark side was still to be determined.

I hoped so.

A piece of white fluff caught my eye and I instinctively snatched it out of the air. The moment my hand touched it, my skin burned. What in Hecate's name…? I strangled a scream as the realization hit me.

Spores.

Princess Buttercup was on all four feet now and her low growl morphed into a far more threatening guttural sound. She wasn't jealous. She was trying to be protective. Why had the window been left open? My family knew the risks.

I glanced at my sleeping niece and it occurred to me that she could've opened it herself. The windows were old and easy to lift. I hurried to the window and slowly shut it so as not to disturb my niece. I didn't want her to wake up and see me battling demon spores that wanted to take over her body. The image might scar her for life.

Another spore floated past me. It was headed for the bed. I needed a weapon. My gaze went straight to the soft Maleficent doll at the end of Olivia's bed. I grabbed the doll and started whacking at the spore. It reminded me of a delicate dandelion seed. When I made contact with the wispy white cloud, it broke into pieces and drifted to the floor.

Another spore appeared behind me. Great Zeus! They were determined little suckers.

I whipped the doll around and made contact. Olivia stirred in her bed and I tried to keep my movements as silent as possible. Not easy when you're cutting through the air with a doll the size of a pillow. The breeze alone was scattering her drawings to the floor. I noticed a picture of stick figures in black clothing and wondered whether she'd been dragged into the Day of Darkness after all.

For a fleeting moment, I thought I had the situation under control until another puff of white caught my eye. More spores? I spun around to see that the window was firmly closed. How were they getting in?

Another one drifted in front of me and I saw that they were coming from the floor. To my horror, I realized the ones I'd batted down were multiplying.

"They're like Hydra!" I said. Cut off one head and two more grow back in its place.

My fingertips itched for lightning. No. I refused to resort to magic for this. I could handle it without using my powers.

But how?

I glanced back at the sleeping child. Charlemagne was awake now, looking at me with curious reptilian eyes. The spores were hardly noticeable right now, but they were there, hovering and waiting for the chance to attach to a body. If I woke Olivia now, maybe I could get her out of the bedroom without a scene.

I reached down and gently shook her arm. "Liv? Nap time's over."

Her eyelids fluttered open and she rubbed the sleep from her eyes. "School was so hard today. I had to color in the lines *and* write my name. My whole name."

"I think Aunt Thora has fresh lemonade for you," I said.

"Pink?" Olivia asked.

"I'm sure she could do a quick spell," I said. Aunt Thora used to make the lemons pink when I was young, until I told her my favorite color was actually blue.

"Okay," Olivia murmured. She stretched and yawned and the python uncoiled.

"Buttercup, go with them," I ordered. I had no idea whether a pod demon could take over a hellhound, nor did I want to find out.

Olivia dragged herself out of bed and I kept one eye trained on her and the other on the hovering spores. Charlemagne seemed to sense danger and stuck close to her feet as she left the bedroom.

The moment she cleared the doorway, I slammed the door closed behind her and turned to face the spores. I rolled up my sleeves, ready to take these little suckers down.

"Do not make me use magic," I ground out. Not for these supernatural snowflakes.

They began to circle me like a spawning tornado. I spun slowly, counting each one. I made it to ten when the door swung open.

"Eden, wildfire!" Grandma's voice rang out.

I dropped to the floor without hesitation. A stream of purple light passed over me and I watched as magical energy fried the spores like insects in a bug zapper. Their delicate forms disintegrated and vanished from the air. Grandma blew off her pointer finger as though it were a smoking gun.

"You're welcome," she said.

I climbed to my feet. "Good aim."

"That's what happens when you play Little Critters," she said. "You get lots of practice for moments like this."

"They're so light and airy," I said. "It makes them tough targets."

She gave me a pointed look. "What makes them tough targets is your unwillingness to use magic."

"I was making progress with Maleficent over there." I gestured to the doll, now facedown on the floor.

"I've seen snails on a highway make more progress."

"Olivia is fine," I said. "The spores are gone." For now.

"That plant is a menace. You need to get rid of it."

"As soon as I figure out how to do it without risking lives and limbs, I will."

"You're risking lives and limbs by doing nothing and letting the seeds spread all over town in the meantime," Grandma said. "Sometimes you have to dispense with the looking and just leap. Your caution is working against you."

"This isn't a game of Little Critters," I objected. "There are real consequences if I handle it wrong." I wasn't above asking for help, but, in this case, the help would mean decimating the whole town.

"What about the dwarf?" Grandma asked. "Doesn't he have any bright ideas?"

"He's not a dwarf," I said. "Neville's a wizard."

Grandma shook her head. "Then he must be a hybrid. Some poor dwarf must've gotten her panties talked off by a silver-tongued wizard."

I pressed my lips together, fighting the urge to lock Grandma in a room full of spores. "Neville is all wizard."

She raised her brow. "You've seen all of him, have you? I thought you were too hung up on the chief. Then again, the dwarf is a supernatural and the chief…isn't."

"Thank you for dealing with the spores," I said. "Now please be quiet."

"Ungrateful spawn," Grandma muttered.

I stomped out of the room. "I won't be home for dinner."

"Why not? Where are you going?"

"Chophouse," I said.

It was time to ask for help.

As much as I hated to drag the supernatural council to Chophouse for an emergency meeting, I knew it was my duty to update them on the situation. They'd need to take precautions and, more importantly, I needed their cumulative years of supernatural experience—Aggie Grace in particular.

A hostess caught sight of me as I entered the restaurant. "Miss Fury, are we expecting you this evening?"

"It's a last minute thing," I said. "Is Rafael here?"

"In the kitchen," she said.

I needed to update him as well because I didn't want any pod demons infiltrating his house either. I knew I could trust him not to panic.

The flamboyant wizard was at the prep table, calmly slicing and dicing onions on the chopping board. My eyes immediately stung. Some fury I was. I couldn't handle cutting raw onions even when someone else held the blade.

"Hey, cousin," I said. "There's about to be an impromptu meeting in the back room. Hope you don't mind."

Rafael gave me a bland smile and moved on to the next onion. "Not a problem. Chophouse is your house. You know that."

"What are you making?" I asked. Through my damp, burning eyelids, I noticed bowls of ingredients already set on the table.

"I'm trying a new recipe," he replied. "I got the idea from a spell I conjured last week. A nice blend of herbs that you wouldn't typically put together."

A 'nice' blend? That description was a bit subdued for Rafael. "I love how your two worlds are so intertwined," I said. "Your work in magic ends up influencing your culinary work."

"I guess it does," he mused. He reached for another onion. "It's not that surprising really. Lots of cutting and stirring in both, isn't there? Although hardly anybody uses a cauldron anymore. They're unnecessarily large and heavy."

I stared at my cousin. Where was his passion? His zeal? "Cutting and stirring?" I repeated.

Rafael continued to slice without his usual finesse. "I think basic culinary skills should be required of any witch or wizard."

"But one does not simply *cut* the eye of newt," I objected. "One must *dice* it."

Rafael stopped slicing and peered at me. "There's more than one way to skin a cat. I can't say the same for an eye of newt." He glanced down at the chopping board. "Or an onion."

Great balls of a minotaur. This didn't sound like my cousin at all. I had the sinking sensation that I was talking to a pod demon.

"Good luck with your recipe," I said. "I should head to the back room before the others get there."

"I'll be in to serve you shortly," Rafael said.

I waved him off. "You know what? It's not our usual monthly meeting so we don't need service, but thanks. You just concentrate on restaurant duties." If Rafael had been taken over, then I certainly didn't want him to overhear any of the discussion and report back to the rest of the invaders.

"Whatever works best for you, Eden," Rafael said. "I'm here to help."

I struggled to keep my eyes from rolling. Rafael would never say that. I mean, he'd help, of course, but he wouldn't be quite so *normal* about it.

I left the kitchen, careful to keep an unhurried pace so as not to alert him to my suspicions. I wove in and out of the tables until I reached the private room at the back of the restaurant where we held our meetings. Despite my efforts to be early, I was the last one to arrive.

"Oh, wow. Everyone's on time," I said. "In that case, we

may as well get right to it." I took a seat between Husbourne Crawley and Aggie.

"No food?" Aggie asked, disappointed.

"Not now," I said. "We need to talk about something important."

"You're darn right," Husbourne said. "Hugh just told me that he's decided to take the potion." Between his pale linen suit, Southern drawl, and wizardly ways, Husbourne was a cross between Gandalf and Foghorn Leghorn.

"*The* potion?" I asked. Hugh Phelps is one of the few werewolves in town that insists on regularly shifting. Other wolves, like my cousins Julie and Meg, take a potion that blocks their transformation.

Hugh stretched his muscular arms. "Why bother? I have an acceptable human form. It seems a waste to switch to something more primitive when I have everything I need exactly as I am. Keeps things simple. I'm all in favor of simple."

Hugh Phelps was content with his human form? More like a pod demon was content with it. This was more bad news. The pod demons had infiltrated more bodies than I realized.

I could feel the weight of Adele's stare from across the table. The matriarch of the LeRoux coven wasn't going to accept Hugh's declaration without an inquiry. It was too out of character.

"You imported a mail order werewolf bride because you're so invested in your werewolf side, but now you're... content to be human?" Adele asked.

Hugh splayed his hands behind his head. "Change is inevitable."

Adele frowned at him, unsure what to think.

Aggie threaded her fingers together. "So what's this emergency meeting about, Eden? If we're not going to order food, let's get this over with. My sister is making a mushroom risotto. If I don't get home early enough, I'll miss out."

My gaze darted to Hugh. I couldn't let him listen to our conversation and report back to the other pod demons. I wasn't sure how it worked—whether there was a telepathic connection between them all or something else. The thought of a growing network of demons made me shudder.

"I know I've bungled this up," I said, "but the truth is, Hugh wasn't meant to be invited."

"Why not?" Hugh asked.

"It's about your wedding gift," I said. "The council is going in on a gift together and we've completely dropped the ball. I was hoping to get it sorted now."

Hugh smiled. "That's kind of you all." He shifted to his feet. "I'll leave you to it then."

"Sorry about the inconvenience," I said.

"No problem at all. It just means more time to spend with my bride." Hugh's long strides took him across the room in a matter of seconds and he closed the door behind him.

"Why not have a group text about the gift?" Aggie asked. "No need to interrupt my artwork for this."

"It's not about a gift," I said. "Hugh's been compromised."

"His behavior is certainly odd," Adele said. "How has he been compromised?"

I explained about the pod demons and the plant I found on the Tasker farm.

Aggie rubbed her temples. "You're telling us that Hugh Phelps has been taken over by a pod demon?"

"I think so," I said. "The Hugh we know is a hardline werewolf. He would never be satisfied with a human body."

"I think Eden's right," Adele said. "It wasn't like him at all."

"There's more," I said.

"More about Hugh?" Husbourne asked.

"No, more pod demons," I replied. "Hugh's not the only

one who's been inhabited." I cut a sympathetic glance at Adele. "I think Corinne has, too."

Adele recoiled. "You can't be serious. Not my grandbaby."

"Have you spent time with her recently?" I asked. "Has she seemed a little...flat?"

Adele bit her lip. "Now that you mention it, I made bourbon raisin bread pudding the other night. It's usually one of her favorites, but she didn't make a fuss over it like she normally would."

"There are others," I said. "And there will continue to be others until we can stop them."

"What do you suggest we do, Eden?" Aggie asked. "We need to prevent these demons from taking over the whole town."

"To be honest, I was hoping one of you might have wisdom to offer," I said. "Aggie, you've been around the longest. Do you have any advice?"

The older Grace shook her head. "I wish I did. They sound positively dreadful."

"What about the mayor?" I asked. "Maybe Husbourne should ask her to issue an alert. Something that requires residents to sleep with their windows closed." Husbourne served on both the regular town council and the supernatural council, so he was our eyes and ears in local politics.

"That might help reduce the spread a little bit," Adele said, "but it won't help those already taken over."

"And how would we explain this to the mayor without revealing too much?" Aggie added.

"We would have to lie, obviously," Husbourne said. "Invent a phony health notice about evaporated chemicals or allergens or some such nonsense."

"Lie to the mayor?" Aggie asked.

"Darlin', we do that every day," Husbourne said. "Wilhelmina Whitehead is a human with no knowledge of the supernatural world."

"Yes, I understand that, but we don't generally resort to bald-faced lies," Aggie said. "We simply skirt the truth."

"I don't see how else we can handle it unless you want to pull back the supernatural curtain," I said.

Adele clicked her perfectly shaped fingernails on the table. "Let's make the request. At least it will help those still unaffected."

"Consider it done," the white wizard said.

"You should know that I think Rafael has been taken over, too," I said. "That's why I asked him not to come in for food and drink orders. I don't know how the demons communicate, whether they'll target us if they realize how much we know."

"What about the FBM?" Husbourne asked. "Can they send in a specialist team? It seems like one agent isn't going to be enough."

"That's not a good idea," I said vaguely. I hated to cause more alarm than I already had.

"Eden, what aren't you telling us?" Aggie asked.

I sucked in a deep breath. "According to our research, the FBM tends to take a scorched earth approach when it comes to pod demons."

Adele drew back and clutched her pearls. "You can't be serious."

"It's rare, but it happens," I said. "Gas explosion. Nuclear radiation. They'll come up with something to explain the tragedy."

"And wipe Chipping Cheddar off the map in the process." Aggie's lips formed a thin line. "We need a better plan than closing windows and swatting at spores."

"I agree," I said. "That's why I'm here."

"You've got to go back to the farm and examine the plant,"

Adele said. "See if there's a way to destroy it that won't back-fire on us."

"What if it's like a weed that doubles down when you uproot it?" Husbourne asked.

"Or just doubles," Aggie added.

"That's the problem," I said. "When I destroyed one spore, it created more. We're not sure what the impact will be if we simply rip the whole pod out of the ground."

"What about Esther?" Husbourne asked. "You said she destroyed the spores in the air with her magic."

Her black magic.

"There's no guarantee it will have the same effect on the pod itself," I said.

"I don't think we should encourage the use of dark magic," Adele said, and I silently thanked her.

"Even when it means saving the town?" Husbourne asked.

"There has to be a way to manage this without requiring the involvement of those wicked witches," Adele said. She cast a sidelong glance at me. "No offense, Eden."

"None taken."

"Let me know when you go back to the farm and I'll go with you," Adele continued. "Any magic I can do, I'm willing."

"Same," Husbourne said.

"Thanks," I said. "I was hoping you'd say that." Although it wasn't a solution, it was a promising start.

CHAPTER TWELVE

I OPENED my eyes the next morning and immediately touched my face and arms. Still inside my body. Phew.

"Your phone has been noisy this morning," Alice said. She drifted between boxes until she reached the bottom end of the mattress. "I hope it's nothing urgent."

"I didn't hear my phone," I said.

"That's because your snores drowned out the sound," Alice said. "You should consider a decongestant."

I reached for the phone on the floor beside me and immediately spotted a text from Neville. Five texts, in fact. He asked me to call him the moment I awoke.

"It must be important," Alice said.

I glanced up at her. "You think?"

"I contemplated waking you, but you're a little scary when you first get up," Alice said.

I clicked Neville's name and waited for him to answer. "Next time wake me, okay? Especially when lives are at stake."

"Thank the gods," Neville said, sounding slightly out of breath.

"What's the emergency?"

"I received a private message from someone on the forum last night regarding the pod demon," he said. "He didn't want to post."

"Why not?" What would be the harm in sharing his information?

"He doesn't want word to get around that his area took matters into their own hands," Neville said. "Too risky."

"So what did they do?" I put him on speaker so that I could get dressed while I listened.

"They're vulnerable to magic-infused fire."

"That makes sense based on what Grandma's magic was able to do to the spores," I said.

"It also explains why the scorched earth approach is favored by officials."

"So we burn the pod and any spores we see," I said. "What about those already inhabited? How do we...uninhabit them?"

"That part is somewhat unclear."

Of course it was. "How so?"

Neville made a noise at the back of his throat. "There were no survivors."

My stomach plummeted. "And how is that different from the FBM's approach?"

"They didn't destroy the area and everyone in it," he said. "Only those inhabited by pod demons. It was a rural area, so it was easier to spin."

"And what was their official story?"

"A tornado," Neville said. "Brought down utility poles and a transformer and started a fire. A dozen people died in the blaze."

I felt nauseous for a fleeting moment, but it passed. I had to focus on the bright side. This was more information than we had yesterday. It helped.

"What's your source's name?" I asked.

"He didn't divulge his real name, only his user name."

"Fine, what's his user name?"

The wizard hesitated. "IDumbleDoreYa."

I nearly choked on my saliva. "We're taking advice from a wizard who makes puns out of Dumbledore's name? Is that wise?"

"He seems legitimate," Neville said. "I checked his other posts on the forum and they all sound reasonable and well-informed." He paused. "Besides, I don't know that we have another choice at the moment. Waiting it out doesn't exactly seem like a viable option."

No, it wasn't.

"Okay," I relented. "I'll assemble a team this morning to join me at the farm."

"Do you think bringing others into the mix is necessary?"

"I spoke with the supernatural council last night and they want to help," I said. "I think we should be as transparent as possible and let them be present when the pod is destroyed. That way there are witnesses and no lingering questions."

"Except for what happens to the occupied bodies," Neville said.

"I don't suppose when the pod is destroyed that the demons fail to survive."

"Afraid not, Agent Fury. The spores will die if they fail to find a host in sufficient time, but there's no evidence to suggest that the demons die when the pod dies."

I didn't think it would be that easy or the FBM wouldn't feel the need to wipe out entire populations.

"Oh, and there's one more thing," Neville said.

"They're allergic to water?"

"No. They can communicate with each other," he said. "It's not quite telepathy. More like a computer network."

"Then it's a good thing we're the cyber crime experts," I

joked. "Thanks, Neville. Great work. I'll let you know what time to meet as soon as I can."

I hurried downstairs for breakfast, feeling reinvigorated and ready to take on the pod demons.

"Are you whistling?" my mother asked. She sat at the dining table with a steaming mug.

"What's wrong with whistling?" I asked. "It's a beautiful day and I'm ready to embrace it." And kill a demon-spawning pod in the process.

"At least whistle something recognizable," my mother said. "That racket sounds like you're calling for Princess Buttercup while trapped under a fallen bookcase."

"That's oddly specific." The smell of freshly baked croissants wafted over to me and my gaze shifted to the oven. "Aunt Thora, did you make homemade croissants?" My day was really looking up.

"I did," Aunt Thora called from a chair in the family room. "They're still warm. Help yourself."

I punched the air.

"And you think I get excited over stupid things," Grandma said as she shuffled into the kitchen.

My mother looked at me intently. "Eden, you're acting strangely upbeat this morning. Are you sure you're all right?"

"Eden's been acting strange since she was old enough to talk," Grandma said.

"Even before that, really," my mother said, "if you count all the times she refused to suckle."

I rolled my eyes. "I wasn't a baby goat. I didn't suckle."

"Exactly," my mother said.

"You really can't blame me for my failure to latch properly," I said. "I was a newborn."

My mother pushed back her shoulders and looked at me. "Then who am I supposed to blame? Certainly not the most

123

perfect bosom in the history of bosoms. My nipples are like bull's-eyes."

Grandma opened her mouth to unleash a witty retort but shook her head instead. "Too many good responses to that. I can't choose just one."

"I'm sure my failure to breastfeed had nothing to do with your body," I said, feeling generous. "Younger women would love to have a body like yours." Operation Kill Them With Kindness was back in effect.

"Don't make your mother's head any bigger than it already is or she'll end up looking like you did the other day," Grandma said.

I poured myself a cup of coffee. "Who made the pot?"

"I did," my mother said. "And I added a dash of devil's claw to the grounds to help with some inflammatory issues I've been having."

Oh, well. Extra creamer and a buttery, flaky croissant would mask the taste.

I stood at the island and bit into the croissant. It was divine. "Am I the only one having a croissant?"

"I'll have one," Grandma said.

"Me, too," Aunt Thora called. "I was waiting for everyone else."

"Not me," my mother said. "I have a date tonight and I can't afford the calories. It'll be fruit and nuts all day until Roger picks me up."

"Who's Roger?" I asked.

"He's an appraiser," my mother said. She wore a demure smile. "And I can't wait to hear how much he values me."

"I'm sure you'll be at the top of his list," I said. I pulled out my phone to text Adele and Husbourne about meeting me at the farm.

My mother studied me. "I didn't hear a trace of sarcasm in that statement."

I took another sip of coffee. "Because there wasn't any. I mean, I don't know who Roger is, but I highly doubt he's been out with anyone like you before."

Grandma walked a semi-circle around me. "You're right, Beatrice. Your daughter is behaving funny."

"What's wrong with being nice and complimentary?" I asked.

"Nothing, except you're a Fury," Grandma said. "We don't do that."

"Pod demons do that," my mother said. She set down her mug with a determined thump.

"I'd look the same even if I were inhabited by a pod demon," I said. "There's no point in examining me."

My mother left the table and moved closer to scrutinize me. "Then how do we know you haven't been abducted?"

"Because I'm standing here," I said. "If I were abducted, I'd be taken away. That's pretty much the definition."

"You know what I mean," she said.

My mother snapped her fingers in front of my face and I pushed her hand away. "Stop."

"Stop because you're a pod demon or because it's annoying?" my mother asked.

"It could be both," Grandma said.

"If I tell you I'm a demon, will you leave me alone?" I asked. "I need to send an important text."

"There's only one way to know for certain," Grandma said. "We have to kill her."

"No," I said. "You really don't."

My mother's hand flew to her hip. "What's the problem? If it's actually you, you'll just come back."

"And if I'm actually a demon, what will happen?" I asked. "We don't know the repercussions." I thought of my efforts to destroy the spores in the guest bedroom. "What if they're like a hydra and two of me come back?"

"Hydra from mythology or Hydra from Marvel's Agents of SHIELD?" Grandma asked.

"Same principle either way."

"When I was a little girl, I wanted a hydra for a pet," Grandma said.

"Most kids want a pony," I said.

"Screw a pony. A pony can't grow back two heads." Her face lit up. "A two-headed pony isn't such a bad idea. Maybe there's a spell…"

I moaned. "Grandma!"

"Eden seems fine to me." Aunt Thora observed me from the family room.

"You always think everyone's fine," my mother said. "You're not as observant as the two of us."

Aunt Thora went back to her crossword puzzle. "Observant enough to see your crow's feet."

My mother gasped and her fingers flew to touch the skin next to her eye.

"Anyway, I'm still me," I said. "Promise."

"These demons are supposed to give people a lobotomy," Grandma said. "Make you act polite and bland, like somebody from Ohio."

"Mother, don't be ridiculous," my mother said. "There are plenty of interesting people from Ohio. Don't you remember that lovely wizard we met from Columbus with the big staff? Now he was far from bland." She looked like the cat that ate the cream—because she probably did.

"Please tell me you're talking about a walking stick," I said. "I just thought it would be a positive change if we treated each other nicely and I decided to be the one to initiate it."

"That's exactly what a demon would say if it wanted to convince us," my mother said, still suspicious.

I walked toward Aunt Thora to seek shelter from the

brewing storm. They weren't letting go of their absurd theory and I had the sinking feeling there was only one way to resolve the argument.

"I'll prove it," I said. "Ask me something no one else knows except us."

"That won't prove anything," Grandma said. "A pod demon has all your same memories."

"Tell them it's me," I urged my great-aunt.

Aunt Thora set her crossword puzzle on the end table. "Since when do they listen to me? My opinion is as irrelevant as yours." She offered an uplifting smile. "Cheer up. Even if they do kill you, it only hurts for a minute and you'll be back soon enough."

"I don't have time to be dead!" I said.

"Oh, Eden," my mother said. "Nobody has *time* to be dead."

"I do," Alice said, popping out of a wall. "All the time in the world, in fact."

"Alice, help me," I said.

"How?" the ghost asked. "I have no way of interfering with their magic."

"Where's Princess Buttercup?" I asked. She wouldn't let them hurt me.

"I saw her sniffing around the barn," Alice said.

"Your precious hellhound can't save you, pod demon," my mother said.

"I'm *not* a pod demon!" I leaned against my aunt on the sofa, not that using her as a human shield would really help. They'd kill us both. I felt like I was eight years old all over again, trying to prevent another punishment after I refused to turn a mean boy in my class into a toad. Kevin McMahon spent a good portion of second grade yanking on my pigtails and other shenanigans. My mother and grand-mother had taught me how to perform minor revenge spells and were furious with me for refusing to use one to defend myself.

"What a waste of talent," my mother had said to eight-year-old me. "If I had your abilities, I'd be ruling half the country by now."

"Why would I want to rule over anyone?" I'd asked. "Absolute power corrupts."

My mother had been appalled. "Where did you hear a ridiculous statement like that?"

"In a book."

I'd been spared that day, but only because my father had come home at the critical moment to announce that he'd bought a new set of golf clubs and my mother had gone ballistic that he hadn't consulted her first. An argument ensued and I escaped. That time.

"You don't even know if killing me will do anything," I said. "What if you revive me and the demon's still there?"

Grandma and my mother exchanged looks and, for a brief, shining moment, I thought I'd won my appeal—until my mother spoke.

"Worth it," she said. Her hand shot out and a bolt of yellow light streaked from her fingertips.

My whole body vibrated painfully for what seemed like an hour before I finally blacked out.

My eyes fluttered open and I stared at the attic ceiling, trying to process what happened and where I was.

Oh. Right. My mother killed me and I was in my own bed. At least they had the decency not to bury me in the backyard.

"Eden?" Alice drifted over tentatively. "Are you...?"

"Alive," I said weakly. Recuperation could take longer for

me than other family members. I hadn't been killed in years. It would likely take a toll on my body.

"Aunt Thora came up to check on you," Alice said. "She left that potion for you." The ghost inclined her head toward the glass on the floor.

I rolled over to inspect it. "That was thoughtful." I sniffed the contents and the scent of lemon filled my nostrils. One of my great-aunt's boost potions would definitely accelerate my recovery.

"I think she feels guilty," Alice said. "She went to her room afterward and didn't speak to the others for the rest of the day."

The rest of the day?

"How long have I been dead?" I sat up and looked for my phone to check the time. Still downstairs, apparently.

"About six hours," Alice said. "They waited to do the revival spell until after they watched that television show they like. The one with the attractive doctors."

My eyes bulged. "They watched a show first?" It really shouldn't surprise me and yet it did.

"They also made margaritas and popcorn," Alice said. "And then your grandmother took what she referred to as a power nap."

Why I thought Operation Kindness was a good idea, I'd never know. Those two were irredeemable.

"Witches," I hissed and headed downstairs to find my phone.

CHAPTER THIRTEEN

THE DAILY GRIND was eerily quiet when Neville and I entered the coffee shop. I'd made plans to meet my helpers at the farm, but I needed a caffeine boost to top off Aunt Thora's potion. The barista stood listlessly behind the counter.

"Good afternoon, Caitlin," I said with as much cheerfulness as I could muster. On the inside, I was still feeling shattered thanks to yesterday's death.

She barely looked up at the sound of her name. "Hello. Your usual?" Her tone matched the flatness in her eyes.

"Yes, please." I glanced at Neville. "How about you?"

He placed his order, his attention fixed on the sluggish barista. Her movements reminded me of a sloth, which was strange because she usually moved at the speed of light.

"It'll only be a minute," she said. "We're not busy."

Neville and I exchanged wary looks. I turned around to survey the rest of the coffee shop. The few customers here seemed dazed and uncommunicative.

"What happened to you?" Neville asked. "I tried to reach

you all day. I thought we'd be heading to the farm before now."

"You don't want to know," I said.

Neville squinted at me. "It isn't wise to be out of contact for so long, especially during a crisis."

"Blame my family," I said.

A middle-aged woman entered the shop and came to stand in line behind us. Based on her running attire and wind-swept hair, she'd come straight from a jog on the promenade that ran alongside the bay.

"Sure is quiet in here," she said. "Makes me feel like there was some catastrophe I don't know about and everyone's in mourning."

"My assistant and I were saying the same thing," I told her.

"It isn't just here," the woman said. "I noticed the same thing along the waterfront earlier. There's a weird lull. One of the things I love about this town is how vibrant it is, but lately…I don't know how to describe it. The energy is off."

"Sleep with your windows closed," I said.

She gave me a funny look. "How's that going to help anything?"

"My sister-in-law is a doctor and she said it's been a weird allergy season," I said. "I think everyone's listless because they're on allergy meds."

"That explains it," the woman said. "I accidentally took the drowsy kind back in college and fell asleep in the middle of a final exam. I never made that mistake again."

"The mayor issued a special alert about it this morning," Neville added. "Have you checked your email?"

"Not for a few hours," the woman said. "Thanks. I'll check it out."

"We need to have Mayor Whitehead send it as a text," I

said, as Neville and I headed back to the car. "Emails will get ignored."

"Did you see the email?" he asked.

"No, I'm about six hours behind on catching up."

"Did your family do a spell to hide your phone?" Neville asked. "I might be able to create a protective spell to prevent that."

Ugh. He wasn't going to stop asking questions until I came clean.

"No, Neville. They didn't hide my phone. What they did was much worse. They killed me."

Neville nearly spat out his chai tea. "They what?"

"Killed me," I said in a low voice. "They were convinced I'd been taken over by a pod demon because I was being too nice."

He stared at me for a long beat. "Agent Fury, I hope you don't take this the wrong way, but your family is severely dysfunctional."

"Tell me something I don't know."

"They cannot murder a federal agent."

I bit back a smile. "I don't think that rule should be limited to federal agents."

"You know what I mean." He seemed genuinely disgruntled.

"It's okay, Neville. They revived me."

His jaw unhinged. "Agent Fury, this is a serious issue and we need to address it. If your family is engaging in that kind of black magic…"

I held up a hand. "I shouldn't have mentioned it." I *really* shouldn't have. "They thought they were helping get rid of a demon. They knew they could bring me back." I dared not add *because they kill each other all the time*.

"Now you're making excuses for them." He shook his head. "This kind of behavior cannot continue."

"You're telling me. My back is going to be sore for a week. I'm sure they dropped me on the way up to the attic."

Neville took another drink and I had a feeling he wished it were more than chai tea in his cup right now. "Are they the reason you didn't want to join the FBM? Because you knew their practices were at odds with…well, most everyone else."

I cast a furtive glance around the sidewalk to make sure we weren't overheard. "I have always wanted to distance myself from them. I managed it for a few years, until my incident with Fergus and the vampire."

"And now you're back in the very town you hoped to escape," Neville said. Sympathy glimmered in his eyes. "It must be difficult for you. Living at home again. Leaving your dream job."

I stared blankly into my cup. "There have been unexpected bright spots."

"Ah. Like Chief Fox?"

I smiled at the thought of the chin-dimpled chief with a heart of gold who could easily pass for an underwear model. Regardless of the state of our relationship, how could meeting Chief Fox *not* be a bright spot?

"And my niece and nephew," I said. "Reuniting with Clara, too." I bumped him with my hip. "And making new friends, of course."

The wizard's cheeks flamed. "You consider me a friend, Agent Fury?"

"Eden," I said. "And, yes, I do."

"It has been refreshing to work with someone so… different from Agent Pidcock."

"I thought you liked Paul."

"Oh, I did," he said quickly. "He was a good wizard and an even better man." He rubbed his thumb along the rim of his cup. "It's just that life here seemed almost stagnant until you came." He seemed embarrassed by his own admission.

"Why do you think that is?" I asked.

"Fishing for compliments, Agent Fury?"

"No, seriously. Why *do* you think that is?" The gears in my mind started to click. "The portal is as dormant as ever. So what's drawing *more* supernaturals here?"

"The vortex?" he proposed. A vortex is a place where multiple ley lines come together, creating powerful energy that can be harnessed. Naturally, Chipping Cheddar had one.

"The vortex has the same energy it's always had," I said. "So why has there been an increase in activity since my arrival?"

He frowned. "Are you suggesting you're the common denominator?"

I finished my drink and tossed it in a nearby trashcan. "What if I am? What if it's my powers? I'd been careful not to use them when I worked for the FBI, but it's been difficult since I came home." I'd been using my abilities more than I'd like since my return to town. Maybe the influx of power had triggered something. Sent up some kind of supernatural flare.

"But recent events," Neville began, "they haven't been simply a matter of creatures coming here for the sake of it. There've been reasons unrelated to you."

"What's the reason for the pod demons?" I asked. "How did that plant end up on the Tasker farm? I thought either Tin Soldiers or Brimstone might be involved, but now I'm not so sure. What if *I'm* the one pulling those things here like a supernatural magnet?"

"I suppose it's possible," Neville said. He seemed to register my disappointed expression. "That's not what you wanted to hear, is it?"

I managed a smile. "Not really, but that's okay, Neville. It's not your job to make me feel better."

"Do you truly believe avoiding your abilities is the best way forward, though?"

"It's a slippery slope," I said. "One day you're changing the color of all the bees in the hive. The next day, you're making their stingers poisonous."

"For what it's worth, Agent Fury, I think you're made of sturdier stuff."

"Never underestimate the allure of powerful magic, however dark," I said. "It calls to you. It will seduce you if you let it."

"You've managed to resist Chief Fox," he said. "I have every confidence you can do the same with dark magic."

"True," I said. "Dark magic doesn't even have a six-pack."

As we reached my car, my phone vibrated with a text from Adele. Her car had a flat tire, so she'd be delayed picking up Husbourne. I replied that I'd pick up Husbourne and meet her at the farm.

"I think you should stay at the office," I told Neville.

"Why?" he asked. "I might be able to offer assistance."

"I think it's safer if we split up," I said. "What if something happens to me, Adele, and Husbourne? You'd be the only one left who knows everything."

"Fair point. Text me the moment you've uprooted the pod."

I gave him a thumbs up before sliding behind the wheel of my car and heading to Munster Close.

Halfway to Munster Close and I was desperate to pee thanks to the latte. My bladder was usually a steel trap. I blamed my post-resurrection body. At least my house was on the same street. I'd make a quick pit stop at home and then grab Husbourne.

As I hurried down the hallway to the bathroom, I recognized Princess Buttercup's faint growl coming from another room. "Buttercup?"

I followed the sound until I arrived in the family room, where Grandma stood encircled by a hellhound, a Burmese python, and a black cat. Candy, my grandmother's familiar, seemed furious. She spat and hissed at the old witch in the circle's center.

"What did you do this time, Grandma?" I asked.

A snarl erupted from Princess Buttercup.

"Animals don't like me," she said simply.

"That's because you let them have food they're not supposed to and they feel sick afterward," I said. "It seems retribution is at hand."

Fiery particles flew from my hellhound's jaws and I realized the situation was more serious than it appeared. To her credit, Grandma remained calm.

"Princess Buttercup," I scolded. "Leave Grandma alone."

The hellhound skulked away, prompting the python to do the same. The black cat remained rooted to the floor, still sparking with vitriol.

"Candy," I said. "What's gotten into you?"

The cat peered at me and swished her tail angrily before stalking off. Grandma sat on the sofa and stared into space.

"Are you feeling okay?" I asked.

"Fine. Why?"

Because I've been here five minutes and you haven't insulted me yet.

"Where's your phone?" I asked.

She cocked her head. "In my purse. Why? Do you need to make a call?"

"Um, no. I just thought you'd be playing Little Critters so you could level up."

Her expression remained unchanged. "Oh, that. I've lost interest."

My eyebrows shot up. "Since when?"

"Since I upset those kids. You're right. It isn't fair. I'm an old woman. I should leave the game to the younger folks."

I folded my arms. "What's your agenda?"

Grandma stared back at me. "What? I can't do the right thing every now and again?"

"Not really." Slowly, I took a step backward. "I'll see you later."

"Where are you going?"

"To the bathroom. That's why I came home."

Her brow wrinkled. "They don't have a bathroom in your office?"

"I'm running errands," I lied.

I tried to appear unconcerned as I headed to my mother's bedroom. The bathroom would have to wait. I found my mother holding up different dresses in front of the full-length mirror.

"Oh, good," she said. "Perfect timing. I'm getting ready for my date with Roger. Which one makes me look younger?" She held a purple dress in front of her body and then switched to a cobalt blue one.

"Younger?" I echoed.

"Yes." My mother looked at me expectantly. "Well?"

"The purple one is more flattering."

She eyed me suspiciously. "What does that mean?"

"It means the color looks better."

"Younger better?"

I rolled my eyes. "Sure. Younger better. Listen, I need to talk to you about Grandma before you go out."

My mother proceeded to change into the purple dress. Bashful she was not. "What about her?"

"I think she'd been taken over."

My mother continued getting ready for her date. "Taken over by what?"

"A pod demon."

My mother cut me a quick glance. "Eden Joy Fury, you know I don't have time for nonsense. I just told you I'm getting ready for a hot date."

"And I just told you that your mother has been taken over by a pod demon. Which is more important?"

She tapped her nail on her chin. "What makes you so sure?"

"She's acting normal."

My mother dabbed perfume behind each ear. "What's wrong with that?"

"Not her normal. Human normal. Like a decent person."

My mother halted and looked at me via her reflection in the mirror. "What did she say?"

"She said it wasn't fair to beat the kids at Little Critters, so she's stopped playing."

My mother sucked in a breath. "That definitely sounds suspicious. I'm going to go ask a few test questions of my own. Then we'll know for certain."

I followed my mother into the kitchen.

"Well, how do I look?" My mother twirled in front of Grandma with a big smile plastered across her face.

"Beautiful," Grandma replied.

My mother's expression fell. "Great Nyx, Eden. You're right."

We stared at Grandma. I didn't think it was physically possible for a demon to wrestle a witch as powerful as Grandma out of her body, yet here we were.

My mother shut the door in Grandma's face.

"She took a nap after we killed you," my mother whispered. "Her defenses were down."

"You mean she took a nap after you celebrated my death with cocktails and junk television," I said.

"Potato. Tomato." My mother clutched her necklace.

"This makes me want to never sleep again. I ought to eat a pound of chocolate-covered espresso beans and wash them down with a gallon of Red Bull."

"Is there a ward we can do?" I asked. "Something to protect us while we sleep?"

"I'll have to think about it," my mother said.

"I need to use your bathroom, then I need to pick up Husbourne. We're headed to the farm to destroy the pod."

"About time," my mother said.

I peed faster than I ever had in my life and exited my mother's bedroom. I caught sight of Aunt Thora as she wandered into the kitchen and decided to check on her. My mother seemed to have the same idea because she followed me.

"Hey, Aunt Thora," I said. "How about some hot water with lemon?"

Aunt Thora smiled sweetly. "You know me so well. A world without lemons isn't a world worth living in."

My mother and I exhaled.

"Aunt Thora, there's something we need to tell you about Grandma," I began.

"What's that?" Grandma's voice cut in and my stomach lurched.

"That you hate lemons," my mother said. "You've been pretending to like them for her sake all these years."

Grandma blinked. "I suppose it's true that I have no strong feelings about lemons, or any other citrus for that matter."

"Sorry to out you," I said.

"Life is simpler without unnecessary drama," Grandma said.

"Can I get that in writing?" I asked.

My mother paled. For once, she seemed incapable of speech.

"I only came in to get a glass of water," Grandma said. "This aging body is dehydrated."

We watched in silence as the pod demon-disguised-as-Grandma poured water from the faucet into one of Olivia's plastic purple cups and shuffled back to her room.

"She used Olivia's cup," Aunt Thora said. "She hates children's cups. She says they're worse than plastic cutlery that comes in colors."

I inched closer to her. "That's not Grandma," I whispered.

Aunt Thora frowned. "What do you mean? Of course it is."

My mother shook her head mutely.

"Pod demon," I whispered.

Aunt Thora's fingers curled around a lemon. "What do we do?"

"Kill it," my mother hissed. "It worked with you."

"It didn't work with me," I said. "I wasn't a demon."

"Says you."

"It's not that simple," I said.

"Nothing ever is with you, Eden," my mother said with a weary sigh.

"Maybe the answer is to do nothing," I said.

My mother's brow lifted. "And let this creature kill your grandmother?"

"Well, Demon Grandma is actually kind of nice," I said. And she certainly wouldn't be using dark magic.

"Are you seriously suggesting letting that thing take over your grandmother's body for your own selfish reasons?" my mother asked, her anger palpable.

"When you put it that way…" I said.

She slapped her hand on the countertop. "Your grandmother wouldn't hesitate to save you if the situation were reversed. So who's the evil one now, Miss Do-Gooder?"

"If I ever needed saving, it would be because of her," I

countered.

Aunt Thora turned to me with a mournful expression. "Eden, you know I love you, but your mother is right. I understand how you feel—your situation is challenging and I'm sympathetic to it—but if there's any way to rescue Esther, then we have to try."

Shame washed over me. "Of course I'll try," I mumbled. "I was only kidding." Sort of.

"We should put Grandma on ice until we can find a way to free her," my mother said.

"Metaphorical ice, right?" I asked.

"Magic ice," my mother corrected me. She shooed me away. "Don't worry. Your aunt and I will take care of her. You worry about rounding up these pod demons and throttling the life out of them…" She trailed off. "Or whatever pathetically humane way you choose to defeat this latest invasion."

"I'll let you know what happens." I started for the door and then twisted back toward them. "Be careful with Grandma. I don't want anything to happen to her."

My mother smoothed her cheeks. "If there's one thing I'm an expert in, it's preservation. Now go do your job before we suffer any more casualties. I don't want these pesky demons to ruin my favorite holiday tomorrow."

"Grandma is in mortal danger and you're worried about the Day of Darkness?"

"Please, your grandmother has spent half her life in mortal danger," my mother said. "Now get out of here so I can get her sorted before my date gets here."

I clenched my hands into fists. "You're still planning to go out with Roger?"

"Well, I have to. He's away next week," she said, as though that justified her decision.

I left the insanity behind before my head exploded and went to collect Husbourne.

CHAPTER FOURTEEN

THE SUN WAS on the verge of dipping below the horizon by the time we met Adele at the designated spot. We hurriedly crossed the field toward the pod's location.

"I brought ingredients for a few spells, in case the first one doesn't work," Adele said.

"I should have changed out of these lighter clothes," Husbourne said. Dirt sprayed up from the ground and smudged the bottom half of his pale yellow trousers.

"Hopefully, this won't take long," I said. "We're about to lose the natural light." I took another step forward and was knocked back by an invisible barrier. "Ouch!"

"What is it?" Adele asked.

"Must be a ward," I said. "I can't walk any further."

"They're pod demons," Husbourne said. "How could they conjure a protective ward?"

A silhouette emerged, nearly indistinguishable from the darkening backdrop. "I created the ward to protect us."

"By 'us,' you mean you and your demon friends," I said. The voice was familiar but too faint to place.

"This town belongs to us now," the silhouette said. "It's

best to give in and not fight the inevitable." The shadowy figure came closer and I gasped when she passed through a beam of moonlight.

"Corinne?" Adele peered into the gloaming at her granddaughter.

The young LeRoux witch focused on Adele. "Mamie, what are you doing here?"

Adele looked at me with an anguished expression. "What do we tell her?"

I wanted to say "the truth," but why bother? Corinne already knew the truth. Well, the demon inhabiting Corinne's body did. The real Corinne was shut down, unable to hear or communicate and if we didn't figure this out soon, she would wither and die.

"Nothing she doesn't already know," I finally said.

"I'm sorry about your tire, Mamie," Corinne said. "I hope you were able to fix it."

"You did that?" Adele asked, aghast.

"I only meant to slow you down so I had time to create the ward," Corinne said. "It seems to have worked."

"Good job on the magic lessons, Mamie," I said sarcastically.

Corinne cocked her head, studying me. "My emotions toward you are complicated. I'm glad I'm able to ease this burden now."

"Ease it how?" I asked.

"We have to help her," Adele said. "Our failure is my granddaughter's death sentence."

"I realize that," I said, but I was at a loss for a useful suggestion. "Try to appeal to her." Although I knew it wouldn't help us or Corinne, it might help Adele—to feel that she did everything she could.

"Corinne, please remove the ward from the land," Adele said.

Corinne shook her head. "I'm sorry, Mamie. No can do. I have to protect the pods."

"There's only one," I said. "I don't think you need to ward an entire farm to protect it. Just post a guard." That I can defeat.

Corinne said an incantation and opened her palm. A spark of light danced above her hand before exploding into brilliance. The white light illuminated the land behind her long enough to rattle me to my core.

"You said there was only one pod," Husbourne said in a hoarse whisper.

"There was."

But not anymore.

Behind Corinne were at least a dozen plants in varying stages of growth. More plants meant more spores and more demons. At this rate, the rest of the town would succumb within the next twenty-four hours.

"Join us, Mamie," Corinne said. "It's more pleasant than you can imagine. I've never felt so at peace."

"At peace?" Adele asked. "You're not yourself. You've been shoved aside in your own body. Your death is imminent. How can you feel at peace?"

"It isn't painful," Corinne said. "In fact, there's no pain at all." She fixed her gaze on me. "I'd been feeling so disappointed lately because of the chief, but that's all melted away now. Life is simple again, as it should be. I'm grateful."

I placed my palms flat against the invisible barrier. "Disappointed why?"

Corinne gave me a pointed look. "You know why."

"You're the one dating him," I said.

"Yes, but we both know he'd rather be dating you," she replied. "Now it doesn't matter. I can accept the relationship for what it is. That's bliss."

"Giving yourself a lobotomy isn't going to make you

happy," I said. "And even if Chief Fox gets booted out of his body, it won't really be him anymore. You'll only be shells." Literal shells of their former selves.

"That isn't love, darling," Adele said. "Why would you want to settle for something so incomplete? I haven't raised you to embrace mediocrity. You deserve better than that."

Corinne approached the barrier. "Love complicates life. When you really think about it, is love even necessary for life? Not really."

Adele reached for my hand and gripped it. I suspected she was trying to stem the rising tide of emotions.

"Love may not be necessary for life, but it sure makes life worth living," Husbourne said.

Corinne scoffed. "You have love in your life, Husbourne? I never would've guessed. You're always alone."

The white wizard didn't flinch. "I don't flaunt my personal relationships, but that doesn't mean they don't exist."

Demon Corinne had a point. I'd grown up on the same street as Husbourne, yet I'd never seen him involved with anyone. It wasn't my business, though. If he wanted to maintain discretion for whatever reason, that was his prerogative.

Adele squeezed my hand before releasing it. "Corinne, listen to me. You're right. A world without love would be simpler. It would certainly mean a lot less pain, but the pain we feel and the sacrifices we make in the name of love… Those are the moments that give our lives meaning and purpose. What's the point of existing purely for the sake of it?"

Corinne's eyes shone in the darkness. "You'll understand soon enough. You all will."

"Well, that's not at all ominous," Husbourne drawled.

I patted Adele's shoulder. "It was a lovely appeal, but she

can't hear you," I said softly. "The demon's in complete control now."

Adele's jaw set. "Then we need to take back the wheel."

"You would have to tear us out, root and stem," Demon Corinne said matter-of-factly.

"Remove the ward and it would be my pleasure," I ground out.

Corinne smiled. "I'm afraid I can't do that.

"Can you break the ward?" I asked. Adele was older and more powerful than Corinne. Given their shared blood and the nature of their magic, Adele should be able to undo Corinne's spell.

"I can try," Adele said.

Corinne wagged a finger. "I wouldn't strain yourself, Mamie. I've engineered it so that I'm the only one who can undo this ward."

"How?" Adele asked. "You haven't developed that kind of magic."

"I had help," Corinne said. "It's amazing what you can learn from one another when you're all connected."

"Grandma," I said quietly.

Adele was visibly shaken. "If she learned a spell from your grandmother, then we're all in trouble."

"Why didn't Esther perform the spell herself?" Husbourne asked. "Why would they have someone less powerful like Corinne do it?"

"My grandmother is incapacitated right now," I said. "Besides, I doubt the demons understand the nuances of our abilities. To them, we're just hosts. And let's face it, they've made it clear that complexity doesn't interest them. They're basically walking, talking amoebas."

"Esther is probably still putting up a fight in there," Husbourne said. "It wouldn't surprise me if the demon failed to wrestle complete control of that wicked witch's mind and body."

I'd had a similar thought but kept it to myself. Optimism wasn't my strong suit.

"In case you decide to be stubborn, Mamie, you should know there's a sting in the tail," Corinne said. "I don't want to see you get hurt."

Adele stepped backward. "That's unfortunate."

My head swiveled toward her. "What is? What does that mean?"

"It means that if you try to break the ward, you'll end up buying the farm in the process," Husbourne interjected.

I knew his statement had nothing to do with the actual farm in front of us.

"Any effort to break the ward will cause intense pain for the participants," Adele clarified.

"Did my grandmother teach you that spell?" I asked. It didn't sound like LeRoux magic.

"No, my mother showed me video tutorials on advanced magic a few years ago," Corinne said. "She wanted to keep your coven away from the annual Rose Festival and devised a plan to lock you on your own property…"

Beside me, Adele closed her eyes in an effort to maintain her composure. "I'd forgotten about that debacle. Thankfully, I put a stop to it before Rosalie could make a fool of herself. I didn't blame Corinne for her mother's harebrained schemes. My granddaughter was young and impressionable."

"And apparently a sponge," I said. "It seems like she absorbed what she learned." I gestured to the barrier.

"Corinne's always been an intelligent young witch," Adele said. "That's why I've always felt it was important to keep her in check."

The three of us observed Corinne, who'd turned and

walked to the rows of pods. She appeared to be talking to them.

"What about you?" Adele asked, directing the question to me. "Your powers are…different. Can you handle this?"

"I'll see what I can do," I said. "But not right now."

"Thank you," Adele said, her gaze back on her grand-daughter.

"Don't thank her yet," Husbourne said. "She hasn't done anything."

Adele watched Corinne's silhouette move amongst the plants. "That's exactly why I'm thanking her."

Husbourne seemed to understand. If I acted now, Corinne could get caught in the crossfire. Whatever I decided to do, I'd need the area clear of innocent victims or I'd risk casualties.

"Then what do we do now?" Husbourne asked.

I continued to watch as Corinne stroked one of the leaves. "Nothing," I said. "The mayor issued the warning and we'll try to protect as many from the spores as we can until we find a way to break through the ward and eradicate the inhabitants without hurting the hosts."

"And them hurting us," Husbourne said.

He was right. Thanks to our interactions with Corinne, the three of us were now targets.

"Take precautions," I said. "The demons will be watching us."

"They'll be more than watching us," Husbourne said. "They'll be aiming to take us over. That's the surest way to stop us from threatening their existence."

I'd been so optimistic when I'd heard from Neville this morning. Things had tumbled dramatically downhill since then. I really hoped this was rock bottom.

We left the farm and I asked Husbourne to drop me off downtown and drive my car home.

"Going to the office?" Husbourne asked.

"Going to work," I said. Right now, that didn't require the FBM office.

He pulled alongside Pecorino Place and let me out. "Good luck, Eden."

Although it was late, the weather was pleasant, prompting many residents to stroll the delightful waterfront streets. I didn't want to call the chief directly and ask where he was because that would raise suspicions. Instead, I shot Neville a text, cringing with every tap of the screen. The wizard kept tabs on the chief as part of FBM procedure. I convinced myself that it was necessary. If the chief of police was now inhabited by a pod demon, Agent Eden Fury needed to know. It was official business, I told myself.

Cheese Wheel thirty minutes ago, came the reply.

So he was off-duty. I couldn't decide if that was better or worse. Would Corinne be with him or was she still at the farm, coaxing more pods to life? I disliked both scenarios.

I sent a second text—this time to Clara. Hopefully, my best friend was still intact. It would be hard to tell from a text exchange, so I invited her to meet me at the bar and kept my tone light and breezy. If Clara was now one of them, I didn't want to give myself away.

With hurried steps, I made my way toward The Cheese Wheel. Everywhere I turned, it seemed as though demon eyes were watching me. As fearful as I was that Chief Fox had been taken over, I had to know for sure. Given the rapid rate of takeovers, it was anybody's guess whether he'd be of sound mind and body. If Demon Corinne hoped to keep him as her companion, it was only a matter of time before she made sure to send a few spores his way. He wouldn't have a clue.

"Eden Fury," a voice said. "We're watching you."

I jerked toward the sound of the voice to see an unfamiliar bald man. Mid-fifties. His stare was as vacant as his body. Whoever this man had been, he was gone—unless I could defeat the pod demons in time.

I kept walking, keeping my head down and avoiding eye contact.

"Eden Fury," another voice said.

And then another.

And another.

"Message received!" I yelled and ran the rest of the way to The Cheese Wheel. I spotted Clara in the parking lot as she emerged from her car. I rushed toward her, plastering a smile across my face.

"What's wrong with you?" Clara asked. "You look weirder with that cheesy smile than you did with a swollen head."

I instantly relaxed. "Thank the gods," I said, and threw my arms around her.

"What's going on?" Clara asked. She pulled back to inspect me. "Did your family do something to you?"

"Yes, but that's not the issue," I said. You know things are dire when you wish you could lay blame at the feet of your evil family.

Clara kept an arm around me as we headed for the entrance to the bar. "Tell me."

As quickly as I could, I filled her in on the latest developments. "And Chief Fox is inside, so I need to see whether the head of law enforcement has changed teams."

She squeezed my arm. "You don't need to pretend for me, Eden. I can feel all the emotions rushing your body. It's a tornado in there."

"The danger is so much worse than I anticipated," I said. "I should've ripped the plant out of the ground when we first discovered it."

"You couldn't have," Clara said. "The risk was too great

based on the limited information you had. You were right to be cautious."

"And look where my caution has gotten us. We now live in Stepford, Maryland." I crossed the threshold and scanned the room for any sign of Chief Fox.

"There, by the jukebox," Clara whispered in my ear.

He was studying the options and, more importantly, he appeared to be alone.

"Would a pod demon care about music choices?" I asked.

"Not from your description of them," Clara said.

"He should know there's an app on his phone, though," I said. "A pod demon might feel the need to look at the actual jukebox."

Clara offered a sympathetic look. "How about you go decide for yourself while I get our drinks?"

"Thanks, that would be perfect."

I snuck up behind him and poked my finger in his back. "Play *I Left My Heart in San Francisco* or you're under arrest."

He twisted to grin at me. "That's an actual song?"

My chest tightened at the sight of his twinkling sea-green eyes. Sawyer Fox was definitely still in there. I felt the tug of the connection between us—it was as strong as ever.

"Seriously? You don't know this classic gem? It's Tony Bennett."

He turned back to the jukebox. "I'll see if he's here."

I pulled out my phone and tapped the screen a few times. "Listen." The song began to play.

"Oh, a slow song," he said. His eyes sparked with interest. "Can't let that go to waste." He extended a hand. "Agent Fury, why don't you show me the proper steps for this classic gem?"

"I don't know…"

"Friends can dance, Fury. I'll show you." He made a few

ridiculous moves that involved thrusting his hips left and right.

"That's not called dancing on this planet, Chief."

He slipped an arm around my waist. "How about this?" He maneuvered us around the makeshift dance floor, swaying gently to the music.

At least I knew if Demon Corinne entered the bar, there wouldn't be a strong reaction to the chief with his arm around me. The current Corinne was closer to a robot than a living creature.

"Where's Corinne tonight?" I felt compelled to ask.

"Don't know," he said. "Didn't ask."

So the chief would rather hang out alone in The Cheese Wheel than check in with the woman he's dating. I guess he wasn't kidding about the casual nature of their relationship.

"Is this where you've been spending your free time?" I asked.

"Here and the bay," he said. "And the river, too. I love the water."

"Same." An image of the chief on a boat with his shirt off sprang to mind and I immediately shut it down. No need to torture myself with those steel abs that were currently pressed against me.

"Did you really leave your heart in San Francisco?" he murmured, and his breath tickled my ear.

"In a bag in the freezer," I said. "I hope no one ignores the Post-It note with my name on it. They'll be in for a nasty shock."

He chuckled. "You have a macabre sense of humor."

"I get it from my family."

He was so close that I could feel the steady clip of his heartbeat. It was a mesmerizing sound and I never wanted the moment to end.

"Have you been sleeping with your windows closed?" I asked.

He arched an eyebrow. "You seem very interested in my sleeping habits, Agent Fury."

My cheeks warmed. "You don't seem to have any allergies."

"I've been diligent, as requested. No matter how many times Corinne keeps coming by unannounced and opening them."

I tensed. "Does she say why she's doing that?"

"She insists I need more fresh air," he said. "She's oddly militant about it. I told her I patrol outside half the day every day, plus I take Achilles for a hundred walks."

"A hundred?"

"Okay, that might be a slight exaggeration, but it's a fair number." He nudged me. "You know how it is. You have Princess Buttercup."

"I know, but she's happy to trot around the backyard when I'm not home. I don't think Achilles has the same temperament."

"No, he likes company and affection and belly rubs." His hand drifted to my lower back. "Much like his human companion." He seemed to realize what he'd done and jerked his hand back to a safer spot.

"I think I could do with more fresh air," I said, breaking apart. "Thanks for the dance. It was nice."

Too nice. I couldn't handle another second with his arm around me, not without doing something I'd regret. The chief was still himself. Mission accomplished. It was time to go home and get a good night's sleep, so I could live to fight another day.

CHAPTER FIFTEEN

I LEFT Clara in the bar to finish her drink. She and the chief both offered me a ride home, which I rejected. I wanted to use the walk home to think. How could I bypass the ward and get to the pods and, more importantly, how could I liberate the inhabited bodies?

As I moved toward the sidewalk, I heard the sound of a familiar voice. I squinted into the darkness and saw Bruce leaning against a car, talking on the phone.

"I told you to take care of it," Bruce said. "I'm a professional and I expect the same level of care from those I do business with." He listened for a beat. "See that you do." He clicked off the phone and looked at me. I noticed that he wore another heavy metal T-shirt. He clearly had a musical preference.

"Is that you, Mr. Fendall?" I asked.

He seemed to notice me for the first time. "Agent Fury, I didn't realize you were a fan of The Cheese Wheel."

"It's an old family favorite," I said. It was true. The drinks at the bar were one of the few things my parents agreed on. I was pretty sure they discussed including visitation in the divorce settlement.

"Are you leaving already?" he asked. "Come on in and I'll buy you a drink. Do my part in support of the FBM."

"I would, but I'm exhausted," I said.

"Maybe next time."

As he started toward the door, a realization took root in the back of my mind and took its sweet time spreading to the frontal lobe.

In support of the FBM.

Bruce had the Sight.

Not only that, but he'd hidden it from me during my last visit. When I showed my badge and identified myself as FBI, he didn't correct me.

I debated how to proceed. Why did he let me believe he was a garden-variety human? Was it because he had something to hide?

"Mr. Fendall, before you go, can I ask you something?"

"I haven't bothered the Taskers, if that's what you want to ask," he said. "I've held up my end of the bargain."

"And I appreciate your compliance." I tried to maintain a friendly demeanor so as not to put him on alert. "Does the name Handel Gottsberg mean anything to you?"

"Never heard of him," he said.

"Are you sure? You haven't used his distribution company to handle any special supplies? Items that might be hard to find around here?" In the human world.

"Can't say that I have."

I pretended to think. "Interesting. Then how did you manage to transport the plant here all the way from Otherworld?"

"What plant?" Although his expression was placid, I noticed a subtle tic next to his right eye.

"The one on the Tasker farm," I said. "Glowing spores.

Produces pod demons that threaten our very existence. Hard to miss."

He laughed awkwardly. "Glowing spores? Pod demons? Are you on any medication the public should be aware of?"

"There's no point in lying, Mr. Fendall," I said. "I know it's you." At least I did now. And here I'd blamed myself. Neville was right all along.

His jaw tensed. "Whatever you're accusing me of—and I'm not claiming to understand—maybe you should take a closer look at Brimstone."

"That's what you wanted, isn't it?" I asked. "You know Brimstone's a demon, so you were hoping I'd write you off as a human and focus on him. It almost worked."

Bruce's expression crumpled. "He's rich and ruthless. I didn't stand a chance of getting the farm with him in the way."

"You didn't stand a chance of getting the farm anyway," I said. "For that you needed the Taskers' agreement and you're never getting it."

He cracked his knuckles. "That's what the pod demon was supposed to help with, but so far it only seems to have taken over the wife. I need the husband."

I closed my eyes and counted to ten in my head. *Deep, calming breaths, Eden.* "You brought pod demons to our town for the purpose of a real estate acquisition. Are you mental?"

No, I could tell he wasn't mental. Just ignorant. Humans with the Sight could often see our world and assumed they also understood it, but that wasn't the case. They weren't steeped in our traditions. They didn't have access to our knowledge. Great Zeus, even the supernaturals in this town were stumped when it came to pod demons.

"What do you mean that they threaten our very existence?" he asked. "Handel said if I planted one on the property, it would only grow there."

"Yes, the pod will only grow there, but that one pod produces hundreds of spores in search of host bodies. My grandmother has been taken over by a pod demon. If I don't get rid of it soon, she'll die and so will countless others." And now for the piece de resistance. "If the FBM gets wind of this, they'll destroy the whole town. Did you know that? So much for Tin Soldiers then, huh?"

He gaped at me for a long stretch, processing the information. "Is it really that bad?"

"It's really that bad, Mr. Fendall," I said softly.

"I didn't mean for this to get so out of hand," he admitted. "I needed something that would remove the Taskers without actually removing them, you know? I didn't want a murder investigation."

"Well, congratulations. What you got is a lot worse."

Bruce closed his eyes and ran a hand over his face. "I didn't understand what a pod demon was. I thought they'd take over the Taskers' bodies and then I could get them to sign away the land and nobody would be the wiser."

"You didn't realize that they multiply at a rate that puts rabbits to shame?"

"Handel said containment wasn't an issue. I was misinformed."

That was putting it mildly. "You were ignorant and stupid," I said. "You've put the lives of everyone in this town at risk, including yourself. Do you realize that?"

"I do now." His head drooped. "What happens now? Are you going to arrest me?" He frowned. "Wait. I'm a human. I don't fall under your jurisdiction."

"You're a human with the Sight who brought a deadly pod demon to the human world," I said. "Trust me. The FBM is interested in you." Unfortunately, I couldn't alert them about Bruce Fendall's crime until after I'd taken care of the pod demon.

He held out his wrists. "If I cooperate, will you promise to request a lighter sentence?"

"Cooperate how?"

"I'll give you Handel. You'll never catch him if he knows you're looking for him. He's like a ghost. I'll get his location."

Even though Handel hadn't intended to unleash deadly demons on the whole town, he'd twice played an integral role in a supernatural crisis in this town and deserved to be punished for his crimes.

"You have a deal," I said. "Now listen. Chief Fox is inside. For the protection of the town, I'm going to have him arrest you right now on a different charge."

"He doesn't have the Sight, does he?"

"No, he doesn't," I said. "He's from Iowa."

Bruce laughed. "You think Iowa is a supernatural-free zone?"

"I assume so," I said. "Everyone there seems so normal." Plus there was no portal close by. No vortex. Nothing to attract supernaturals. Although if I were a Sighted human, I'd move there just to get away from the world that was hidden in plain sight.

"Don't you think it would be helpful if the chief of police knew how special this town is?" Bruce asked. "It would make your job easier, I'd think."

"Not if I have to protect him," I said.

"Knowledge is power," he countered.

"Knowledge can also be dangerous," I said. "It makes you vulnerable. A target." Like with the pod demons.

"That's a paternalistic attitude," he said.

"I'm not really interested in your opinion, Mr. Fendall," I said. "You play along with me now, and I'll help you when the time comes."

Bruce nodded. "Nothing too terrible, right? Maybe I tried to sell you drugs?"

I pulled out my phone and texted the chief. "Drugs it is."

The chief didn't seem at all miffed to have his evening off interrupted. He thanked me and drove Bruce to the station for processing. I was so tired by then that I agreed to let Clara drive me home.

"Chief Fox looked good tonight," she remarked. "He's got some smooth moves on the dance floor."

"I shouldn't have danced with him," I said, feeling sullen. "It just reminds me of what I can't have."

"Listen, I know you feel obliged to keep that protective wall between you," she said. "I mean, you tried that with me, too, and you can see how that worked out for you." When I left Chipping Cheddar to attend college and then work for the FBI, I'd let my friendship with Clara fade. It had been deliberate on my part. I'd hoped to distance myself from my family and, in turn, from my true nature and Clara was one more reminder of the real Eden. Now that I was back, however, it seemed pointless and stupid. Clara had always been a good friend and she deserved better.

"Clara, you know it had nothing to do with you…"

She silenced me with a look. "Of course, I know. I've known you forever and I know the truth about you, so I understood, but Chief Fox is oblivious."

"Good. That's how he should be. It's safer."

"For him? Or for you?"

I exhaled loudly. "Is this where you tell me to listen to my heart?" I asked. "Because you and I both know the world doesn't work that way." As an empath, Clara struggled with intimacy. She found relationships and the resulting emotions too overwhelming.

She pulled into the driveway and let the engine idle. "I think you should tell him the truth. Don't let your family scare you into believing he'll reject you, or you'll endanger him. That's their way of controlling you."

"The ultimate pod demons," I joked.

"This pod demon situation is pretty serious, huh?" Clara asked.

"Gee, what makes you say that?" The sarcasm slipped out before I could stop it.

She offered a sympathetic smile. "The fact that the Day of Darkness is tomorrow and you've barely complained about it. If I recall correctly, it's your least favorite holiday."

"It's not a holiday," I insisted. Not mine, anyway.

"Well, if you need a place to hide from the madness tomorrow, you can always come to my place."

"I appreciate the offer, but with Grandma on ice, my mother is going to be on a rampage," I said. "She won't let a life-threatening pod demon get in the way of her special day."

"I'm here if you need me," Clara said.

"You're the best," I said. She really was. What a moron I'd been to cut myself off from a friend like Clara.

I exited the car and plodded into the house, acutely aware of the weight of fatigue. Downstairs was quiet, so I climbed the attic steps and changed into shorts and a T-shirt before collapsing on the mattress. As much as I wanted to avoid sleep as a preventative measure, I was simply too exhausted.

I also wanted to escape the parade of thoughts marching through my mind. Sleep would give me a reprieve. The Day of Darkness had plagued me as a kid and escaping Chipping Cheddar had granted me freedom from the celebration until now. Dread crept from toes to my legs and then spread through the rest of my body. I yawned and my body begged to curl into a ball and rest.

"I'll watch over you," Alice said. She emerged from the wall and hovered beside the mattress. "If I see any spores, I can wake you."

"Are you sure? I don't want you to stage an all-night vigil."

"Why not? I'm a ghost. It's not like I have an early morning appointment."

I fluffed the pillow beneath my head. "That would be helpful, Alice. Thank you."

"Sweet dreams, Eden."

"From your lips to the gods' ears." I rolled onto my side and let sleep take me.

CHAPTER SIXTEEN

I OPENED my eyes and relief swept over me. I was still in the attic. Still conscious. I turned to look for Alice in order to thank her and swallowed a cry when I saw the body next to me on the mattress.

It was mine.

I froze, uncertain what was happening. Alice was nowhere to be seen. I scrambled off the mattress and fled downstairs. The kitchen was surprisingly empty. There was almost always somebody in the kitchen, though our numbers had dwindled thanks to the recent departure of Anton and his family.

A quick glance at the microwave clock explained the absence of the wicked witches. Six o'clock in the morning was far too early for them to rise, even on a day as venerated as the Day of Darkness. Unfortunately, there was a body upstairs that looked like me that I couldn't ignore. I was going to have to wake someone. But which someone? As much as it pained me to admit it, my mother was handy in a crisis.

Her bedroom door was open, so I slipped into the darkened room and hurried to her bedside. She wore an eye mask and I heard a slight wheeze as she breathed.

"Mom," I said.

No answer.

I decided to raise my voice. "Mom!"

She didn't move. I reached for her arm to shake her awake, but my hand sliced right through her. What in Hecate's name?

I tried again with the same results. Shock tore through me. Why was I incorporeal? Was this a stress dream? It wouldn't surprise me, given recent events. A worse idea hit me.

Was I dead?

I rushed from the bedroom and called for Alice. If I were dead, she'd still be able to communicate with me. She'd be the only one in the house who could.

"Alice," I shouted again.

"Eden?" The ghost materialized out of thin air, as ghosts were wont to do. Her eyes narrowed as she took in my appearance. "Are you unwell? You seem a little…flimsy."

"I think I'm a ghost," I said, panic bubbling to the surface. "I think I'm dead, like really dead."

Alice regarded me for a moment. "No, I don't think so."

"Why not? I'm incorporeal. I tried to touch my mother's arm and my hand went right through her."

"But I saw you asleep upstairs not long ago," Alice said. "You were fine. Sleeping soundly."

"Go check again."

She frowned. "What do you mean?"

"I mean go to the attic and check again."

Alice's form dissipated but only for a moment. She returned quickly, her eyes round with fear. "You just woke up."

"No, I woke up next to…"

The sound of footsteps startled me. I turned to see...me. Demon Me. My doppelgänger went straight into the kitchen the way I usually do. She didn't seem to notice us.

"Why can't the demon see us?" I asked.

"If I had to guess, I'd say it's because you're more than the sum of your parts," Alice replied.

"In English, please."

"Your body alone isn't what makes you a fury," Alice said. "It's all of you. In other words, Demon You is missing crucial bits."

"In that case, doesn't that mean I *am* the sum of my parts?"

Her expression turned puzzled. "Well, never mind that. Let's focus on the priorities."

"You mean priorities like what in the hell happened?" I asked. "Why didn't you stop the spores? How did they get in?"

Alice's brow creased with regret. "I'm so sorry. I heard music coming from outside and went to investigate. It was such an odd hour for Taylor Swift and I was worried that there was some kind of invasion on the way.

"And they were playing *Shake It Off* to announce their arrival? They're not a high school marching band, Alice. They're pod demons."

"It turned out to be Michael, the new neighbor," Alice said. "His car was running and the song was on the radio. I noticed his golf clubs in the back, so he must have an early tee time and ran back into the house for something."

I wasn't much of a crier, but phantom tears welled in my phantom eyes.

Alice hung her head in shame. "It must have happened while I was gone. It wasn't very long."

"Long enough," I said. "You didn't see me leave my body?"

"No."

I heard a cabinet open and close and went to the kitchen to see what Demon Me was doing. She filled a bowl with Cheerios, but instead of using milk, she added water from the tap.

"Yuck. That's disgusting," I said. "I would never eat that." At least if my mother or Aunt Thora saw what I was doing, they'd know it wasn't me.

"They must need a lot of water," Alice said. "They grow from plants, after all."

"This is a nightmare," I said.

"I don't think it is," Alice countered. "How would I be experiencing it with you?"

I heaved a sigh. "I don't mean an actual nightmare."

"Well, if it's any consolation, I don't think you're dead," Alice said.

"Why not?"

"Because it sounds like you didn't experience any of the death hoops or you'd have mentioned them by now."

"Death hoops?" I repeated. "What? Are there literal flaming hoops I need to jump through to reach…the next place?"

Alice tapped her foot impatiently. "If I'd reached the next place, I wouldn't be here now, would I?"

"About that…" I began, but this wasn't really the time to discuss Alice's earthbound spirit.

"Let me ask you this—did you see a white light?" Alice asked.

"No."

"See any loved ones who'd already passed on?"

"No, but I saw one who passed gas. My hand went right through her arm, though."

Alice cringed. "Yes, it's an unfortunate byproduct of being invisible. You see and hear a lot more than you'd like. You really don't want to know what your mother gets up to, even when she's alone."

I held up a hand. "I really don't." I wracked my brain to come up with an answer. "So if I'm not dead, what am I? In purgatory?"

"I think you'll have to ask someone with more knowledge of these things."

"That someone will have to be able to see and hear me," I said. "Kind of a problem right now." Still, I had no choice but to try and communicate. "When you disappear, how do you do it? Do you just wish to be in another place and you get transported there?"

"Do these look like ruby red slippers to you?" She clicked the heels of her old-fashioned black boots.

"Hey, when did you watch *The Wizard of Oz*?"

"You said it's a classic. When I saw it was on, I took advantage of the opportunity." She shivered. "Those flying monkeys are the stuff of nightmares."

I cut a quick glance at Demon Me as she took a sip of tea and her lip curled. She set the cup on the counter and proceeded to dump two more spoonfuls of sugar into the mug.

"If I don't get my body back soon, I'll end up with diabetes."

In the distance, I heard a toilet flush and I waited to see whether my mother or Aunt Thora would realize that I'd been taken over.

My mother padded into the kitchen first. "You're up early. Must be all the excitement for the Day of Darkness." My mother shivered. "I can't wait to soak up all that magical energy."

"I'm happy if you're happy," Demon Me said.

"That's sweet," my mother replied.

I flung out my hand. "Oh come on! I would never say that,

Mom. You know I don't care if you're happy!"

"Maybe after wrongfully killing you, she's decided to exercise more caution," Alice suggested.

Aunt Thora must've slipped into the backyard unnoticed because she entered the house through the back door with a basket of lemons in her hand. "My lemons must know it's a special day. Their color seems more vibrant than usual." She lifted one to her nose and inhaled its scent. "It's like a citrus drug."

"I can't wait for you to put on your dress," my mother told Demon Me. "You're going to love it."

"What about Esther?" Aunt Thora asked. "Are we going to…wake her?"

My mother chewed her lip. "I'm not sure what to do about that. We need her for the photos."

"Are you kidding me?" I yelled. "You do not need to de-ice Grandma for the sake of photos." This took 'keeping up appearances' to a new level.

"I think we should include her," Demon Me said.

Aunt Thora shot the demon a quizzical look. "You do?"

"It's a family photo on one of the most special days of the year," Demon Me said. "It won't be the same without her."

Ugh. Liar!

"Eden, honey. Why don't you go and get dressed?" my mother asked. "That way if we need to make any adjustments to your outfit, we have plenty of time. First ritual starts in two hours."

"Sure. I'm finished eating now."

My mother wrinkled her nose. "You ate food on a morning like this? Well, I suppose I can't expect miracles. Just suck in if you have to."

Demon Me retreated to the attic to change.

"They didn't notice," I said, more to myself.

"You've lived away for years now," Alice said. "They're not as used to you as they are to each other."

"I'm her child," I said. "Wouldn't you notice if your child had been commandeered by a demon?"

"I don't know," Alice said quietly. "I never had children."

My tightly wound phantom body relaxed at the sight of Alice's pained expression. One of these days, I'd get her whole story.

I turned and followed my doppelgänger upstairs. She moved mechanically, as though she were still getting accustomed to having limbs.

"Are you wearing the outfit?" my mother called a few minutes later.

"Yes, Mom," Demon Me called from the attic. "I'll be there as soon as I brush my hair."

Alice and I observed Demon Me as she stood in front of the mirror, not quite able to believe I was about to be photographed in that dress. The neckline was provocatively low and the deep black fabric washed out my pale skin. Although I'd said no lace, apparently my mother had overruled me because the edges were trimmed in lace, including the neckline. Photographs last forever. If I let them capture that image of me, my family would lord it over me for the rest of my eternal life. Not a comforting thought.

"She looks like an old-timey prostitute at a funeral," I said.

Alice inclined her head. "Eden, your clothes."

"I know. I thought that's what we were just criticizing."

"No, the ones you had on," Alice said. "They've changed to match the demon's."

I glanced down at my outfit. Sure enough, I was no longer in my blue T-shirt with the image of a cat eating tacos.

"So I have to wear whatever my demon counterpart is wearing?" Sweet gods above, I hope she didn't buy me a new wardrobe. Or worse, raid my mother's closet.

"If it makes you feel any better, I think you look alluring and mysterious," Alice said.

"That demon doesn't know how I part my hair," I said. "She's gone too far to the side." I touched my head and, sure enough, my part had shifted. That was going to bug me all day.

"She missed a button on the bodice, too," Alice said.

Ugh. The ghost was right. The tops of my boobs were peeking out. "I can't let me out in public like that."

"I think you have bigger priorities at the moment," Alice said.

"Can't I combine my priorities?" I asked. "If I get rid of the demons before I have to leave the house, then maybe I can avoid being seen in public in that outfit."

Alice observed Demon Me with interest. "Why do you think she can't hear me? She's still you."

"She's not all of me, though, not if this" —I waved my hands in front of me— "is walking around out here."

"So you took your powers with you?" Alice asked. "Seems unlikely."

"I don't think I took them because Demon Corinne still had access to magic," I said. "I think it's because they're generally simple creatures. Their main goals are to multiply and survive. My powers might be too complex for this demon to access."

"And Demon Corinne only used magic when they felt it was necessary to protect the species' goals," Alice said, seeming to understand.

"Magic and powers don't hold any interest for them unless they serve as the means to an end," I said. "They really are single-minded."

Demon Me headed for the stairs and I trailed behind, careful not to move too quickly and stir up a breeze.

"Eden," my mother said, as I entered the kitchen. Her gaze

traveled over me. "You look surprisingly sexy. I didn't think it was possible. A little more makeup wouldn't do any harm."

"Which colors do you suggest?" Demon Me asked.

"Why don't you let me do it?" my mother asked. "Smoky eyes would look amazing on you. Not as amazing as my eyes, of course, but still worth doing."

"I'm in your capable hands," Demon Me said.

I couldn't listen to another word. My own mother failed to recognize that wasn't me. The same mother who killed me for being too nice. What a world.

I started to walk away.

"Eden," Alice called. "Where are you going?"

I craned my neck to look at her. "To get help," I said. "If there's even a ghost of a chance that Neville can see me, I have to try."

CHAPTER SEVENTEEN

I MADE it as far as the driveway, debating the options. I couldn't drive a car if my hands and feet couldn't make contact with the steering wheel and pedals. What other mode of transport...?

Right. Problem solved.

Large black wings fanned out behind me. They were the fury trait I'd inherited after accidentally using my siphoning power in San Francisco. I tended to keep them under cloak and key, but now seemed like the perfect time to make use of them. I launched into the air and headed for the office. Knowing Neville, he was already there, diligently trying to find a solution to our pod problem.

The town looked so peaceful from the vantage point of the sky above. In the distance, the lighthouse stood head and shoulders above the other buildings. People were driving to work and to school, but it wasn't a mad dash. More of a leisurely pace. Chipping Cheddar was rarely congested. That level of busy mostly occurred at the height of summer when the tourists swarmed the town to enjoy the waterfront life-style. My heart seized as I thought of the visitors that might get caught in the crossfire if the town had to be decimated. So many lives were at stake, all because of Bruce Fendall's greed and his ignorance of the supernatural.

I zeroed in on the office and lowered myself straight into the building through the roof, landing near the back table where Neville liked to tinker with inventions. As anticipated, Neville was already hunched over his desk, typing away on the keyboard. I tucked away my wings and went to see if he'd unearthed any valuable intel.

I leaned over his shoulder and read the article headline —*Ten Spells Every Wizard Must Learn Before Age 30.* "How about the spell that allows you to see and hear whatever I am?" I asked.

Neville slipped out of his chair and fell on the floor. "Agent Fury! Where did you come from?"

My phantom heart thumped wildly. "Neville, you can hear me?"

He twisted to peer up at me from his spot on the floor. "Why wouldn't I be able to hear you?"

"Because I'm a ghost?" I demonstrated my apparitional skills by slicing my hand through the back of his chair.

He blinked rapidly. "You're not a ghost."

"That's what Alice thinks, too, but when I woke up, I wasn't in my body. The demon was."

The wizard staggered to his feet, still fixated on me. "Why are you dressed like you're attending a Spanish Inquisition?"

"Because it's the Day of Darkness and Demon Me is following my mother's sartorial orders like some kind of witchy soldier."

"You didn't wake up in this dress?" His eyes drifted to the exposed part of my chest and I snapped my fingers.

"Eyes up here, Rover."

Neville's head snapped back to eye level. "Sorry," he mumbled.

"I woke up in the clothes I slept in, but when the demon changed her clothes, my appearance changed, too."

"That's helpful," Neville said. He seemed to have recovered from the shock. "I believe you're an astral projection."

"That's an out-of-body experience, right?"

"More or less," Neville said. "You've projected your 'self,' or your consciousness, from your physical form, except you're still attached to your physical body. The cord hasn't been severed yet."

Yet.

"How did this happen?" I asked.

"I suspect when the demon took over your body, your consciousness reacted by vacating the premises," he explained. "It's probably a benefit to be able to have your consciousness walking around outside your body. It might stave off the effects of the demon's inhabitance."

"Well, that's good for me, but it doesn't help everyone else."

"No, but the fact that you can still retain agency…" Neville nodded, more to himself. "This is a plus."

"Speak for yourself," I said. "You're still in solid form."

"Have you never used astral projection before?" Neville asked. "No dream walking?"

A memory came to me. I was eleven. I was with a group of friends in the woods, playing hide-and-seek. I'd squeezed inside the base of tree to hide. It was such a good spot that no one could find me. Eventually, darkness settled over the forest and I got scared. I remembered going in search of my friends to see if anyone was looking for me. I found them in a clearing as they split up to hunt for me. I jumped up and down and called to them, but no one noticed me. I followed one of them as he sniffed his way to the tree I'd hidden in—he was a werewolf.

"Found you," he'd said, and my eyes had opened to peer at

him in the darkness. I was back in the base of the tree. I'd assumed that I'd grown so bored waiting to be found that I'd fallen asleep.

"I thought it was a dream," I murmured.

"Why do I have to wear the same clothes as Demon Me?" I asked. I really wanted out of this dress. It itched and it wasn't even real.

"It makes sense," he said. "You're a projection of yourself, after all."

"I guess it doesn't work the other way around," I said. "When I sprouted wings, I doubt Demon Me felt the pinch."

"It's unlikely the demon feels much of anything at all," Neville said. "Even if it does, it might not understand the implication."

"Let's hope not."

"We'll have to add this to your list of abilities," Neville said.

On the bright side, it wasn't a new power. It was one I simply didn't realize I possessed because I'd suppressed it.

"Let's wait until I'm back to normal before updating my list," I said. "Speaking of normal, why can you see me?" That didn't seem normal to me.

"It's the office," the wizard said. "I have several wards installed, including one that reveals invisibility spells. It's not that you're invisible in the usual sense, but the ward isn't designed to recognize nuances. The key principles still apply."

"So you won't be able to see me outside of the office?"

"Not yet." He hustled to the table at the back of the office, "but I can change that."

"What are you going to do? Ward the whole town so everyone can see me?" I joked.

"That wouldn't be wise," Neville said. "Imagine the questions it would raise to see two federal agents wandering around town. It would also give the pod demons a reason to act against your physical form. Even single-minded creatures will take action to protect themselves from extinction."

"They'll destroy my body if they see me as a threat?"

Neville nodded. "That would remove the threat, wouldn't it? You'd be dead. As far as they know, you've succumbed like every other resident who's been inhabited. Now you can continue to work against them without alerting them."

"It's going to be you and me against the world if we don't finish them off soon." That was a horror story I wanted no part of. "By the way, we can thank Bruce Fendall for this mess." I updated him on last night's events.

"You see, Agent Fury," Neville said. "There was a logical reason that pod ended up in town that had nothing to do with you. Perhaps you're not the magnet for trouble you think you are."

He was right. The pod demons didn't choose to come here. They were brought here as part of a business tactic. My presence, the portal, the vortex—all a coincidence. It was a relief to know I hadn't caused this crisis.

Neville began pulling materials off the shelves. "I remember this one time at wizard camp…"

"Wizard camp?"

He hastened a glance at me. "You didn't go to camp?"

"Do you seriously think I'd have gone to supernatural camp? I'd rather have slit my throat."

"Well, I happened to adore camp," Neville said. "Where do you think I developed my interest in botany?"

"Friday nights when you were home alone and everyone else had plans?"

He cocked an eyebrow. "My, my. Astral Eden has a rather tart tongue, doesn't she?"

"I never went to camp," I said dully.

"Anyway, this one time at Camp ChickaMerlin…"

I barked a short laugh. "Your camp was called Chicka-Merlin? Why not just Merlin?"

"I didn't name the camp, Agent Fury. I simply attended it." He opened a small box and retrieved a plain silver band. "Anyhoo, I had a friend at camp called Franklin and one of Franklin's favorite pranks involved astral projection. He would pretend to be asleep. Meanwhile, he'd be running around the campground, wreaking havoc."

"He could touch things?" I made another attempt to make contact with a solid object, but my hand went straight through the table.

"Franklin embraced his abilities," Neville said. "He honed the skill over time. So a few of us got together after Franklin had short-sheeted our beds one too many times and devised a spell to pierce the veil, as it were, and be able to see him."

"And you were successful?"

"Naturally. That's when I acquired the nickname, Neville the Devil."

I coughed to cover a laugh. "Neville the Devil?"

He shook a pair of pliers at me. "Don't laugh, Agent Fury. Piercing the veil was considered the devil's work."

"Only because they'd never met my family."

Neville turned his attention to the ring. "I need to fashion myself a charmed object, similar to your invisibility locket. Only this one will allow me to see and hear you outside of this office."

"Will it take long?"

"Not for me," Neville said. "Why do you think the FBM pays me the moderate bucks?"

"I'm putting in for a raise for you, Neville," I said. "As soon as I'm corporeal again."

"You're too kind." He reached for a mortar and pestle. "As long as I wear the ring, that should allow me to carry on communicating with you."

"You're so much cooler than Q," I said. "James Bond would be lucky to have you."

"And I would be lucky to have access to the British Secret Service's research and development budget, but hey ho." Neville shrugged. "Luckily, I can work my magic on a budget."

Small mercies. "We have to put a stop to them, Neville. They keep multiplying. Alice only left her post for a few minutes and I was invaded."

Neville pushed up his glasses before they could slide to the end of his nose. "I have an idea, but I'm going to have to enlist help."

"From whom?"

He lowered his gaze. "You're not going to like it."

Nausea rose in my throat as the realization washed over me. "How can I object? Desperate times call for desperate measures."

I stood beside Neville on the front porch of my house as he knocked on the door. "I wish my mother and I had a secret word," I said.

"It would be useless in this scenario because your doppel-gänger would know it," he said. "The demon isn't just someone who looks like you, it *is* you."

Good point.

The door opened, revealing my mother in her own Day of Darkness dress. With her wide-brimmed black hat and black silk gloves, she looked ready to attend a royal vampire wedding. The body-skimming dress was more risqué than mine. No surprise there.

"Mr. Wyman, can I help you?"

At least she remembered his name.

"May I speak with you alone outside?" he said. "It's an emergency."

My mother tried to frown, but her forehead didn't comply. She must've dipped into the anti-aging potion again. "What's this about?" She stepped onto the porch and closed the door behind her.

"Eden's been compromised," he said. "You have another pod demon in your house."

She eyed him suspiciously. "How do you know?"

"Because the real Eden is right here on the porch," he said. "She's astral projecting." He removed the ring from his finger and handed it to her. "Put this on and you'll see."

My mother slipped the silver ring on her finger and gasped at the sight of me. "I can't believe it! Your makeup looks just as good in ghost form. My handiwork is exquisite."

I rolled my eyes. "Not really the focus, Mom."

"I should've known it wasn't you," she said. "You were far too agreeable. It didn't feel right."

"I want you to act like you don't know," I said. "Let me participate today as is."

"And why would I do a thing like that?"

"Because I don't want to rouse suspicions and because I need you to do a few things for me. For starters. I'm going to use my astral form to cross through the ward at the Tasker farm and I need your help to do it."

My mother folded her arms. "Eden Fury needs my help. Again. Getting to be a habit, don't you think? At what point will you acknowledge that black magic is useful?"

"I don't deny that it's useful," I said. "It's the price we have to pay for it I object to."

"What do you need me to do?" she asked.

"Tell Aunt Thora to stay here and make sure Grandma and Demon Me don't leave the house."

"Easily done," my mother said.

"Then give Neville back the ring and come with us to the farm," I said. "He'll explain the rest in the car. He's in charge. Whatever he says, you do it."

"He couldn't have made more than one ring?" my mother asked.

"He's kind of working on short notice," I said.

My mother removed the ring and begrudgingly gave it back to Neville. "I'll be right back."

Neville and I returned to his car and my mother emerged from the house a few minutes later. She started to get in the passenger's side but Neville stopped her.

"Eden's sitting there."

My mother peered at the seemingly empty seat. "You need to get in back, Eden, honey, or we'll look ridiculous."

"Has she looked in a mirror this morning?" I asked.

"Eden wants to know if you've looked in a mirror," Neville said.

I tried to smack him but my hand went through his arm. "You're not supposed to repeat everything I say."

"Sorry," Neville mumbled. "It was automatic."

He backed out of the driveway and we headed to the Tasker farm. "I doubt Corinne's there now. It'll just be the ward we have to contend with."

Unfortunately for Neville, he had to contend with my mother's radio preferences. Every time he chose a station, she would change it in search of a better song.

"I don't do country," she proclaimed, changing the channel yet again. She settled on an Alicia Keyes song and belted out the lyrics to *Girl On Fire*. Finally, Neville turned off the radio in order to explain the rest of the plan.

"You're finally straying from your no-kill policy," Neville said.

My mother's eyes brightened. "She is? Oh, this is the *best* Day of Darkness gift *ever*."

"I don't see that I have a choice with this one," I said. "If I don't kill these pods, the demons will kill everyone in town—or the FBM will come in and do it for us."

"Oh, I've dreamed of a moment like this," my mother said. She couldn't disguise her expression of pure joy and I wanted to vomit, though I doubted it was possible in my current state.

"You've dreamed of trespassing on a farm and destroying plants?" Neville asked.

"It's not trespassing, darling," she said. "This is open season on pod demons and my daughter is at the helm, ready to deal them cards of sweet vengeance. Happy days, indeed."

"I'm eradicating an invasive species to save the town, not indulging my inner evil," I said. "Tell her that."

"I'm not getting in the middle of family squabbles," Neville said. "I'm only acting as a conduit for the sake of the mission."

We reached the edge of the farm and Neville parked off the road between two large oak trees in case any pod demons happened to drive past. We approached the field with caution.

"Mind the ward," Neville said.

My mother stepped right into it, stubbing her toe. She winced. "A little more of a warning next time."

"No sign of Corinne," I said. No sign of anyone except the pods.

"I wish I could watch you in action." My mother glanced around awkwardly, not sure where I was standing. "Could I just wear the ring for the big moment?"

"Don't give her the ring," I warned. "I need you to be my eyes."

"I'm afraid I can't do that," Neville said.

My mother's eyes narrowed. "She told you to say that, didn't she?"

"Tell her to get ready," I said.

"Get ready, Mrs. Fury," Neville said.

"Get ready for what?"

I placed a hand on her shoulder and concentrated on siphoning as much magic as I could without depleting the both of us. I wasn't sure how this influx of magic would impact my astral form. I couldn't afford any mistakes.

My mother's legs began to slide out from under her. "Neville, help her," I said.

I turned and ran straight through the ward, Corinne's spell unable to block my astral form from crossing the threshold. Magic thrummed within me and I felt the immense pressure of it, a dull ache in my incorporeal chest.

I skidded to a halt in front of the rows of pods. New spores were in the process of forming.

"No green thumb? No problem."

I aimed both hands and released my mother's wildfire. Purple light streaked from my fingertips and attacked the pods. I watched with satisfaction as the glowing spores dissipated into puffs of purple smoke. Each pod then exploded, tearing up the earth around them. Dirt flew through me and splattered on the ground. The roots, now exposed, sizzled with the wildfire's last gasp.

I felt an amorphous pang as the remaining pod disintegrated, likely an echo of what my actual body was feeling right now. I wondered whether the inhabited bodies would register the death of the pods as well. If they were connected to each other the way we believed, then the answer had to be yes.

I stared at the scorched earth for a prolonged moment. Disappointment stirred. Part of me had hoped that this would be enough. That I'd destroy the pods and snap back into my body. No such luck.

I silenced the overachiever in me. The pods were gone.

This was a huge step in the demons' defeat. I crossed the field and walked back through the ward to where my mother and Neville awaited me. I'd celebrate when the deed was fully done.

"I think I have it figured out," I said.

"How to look good while astral projecting?" Neville asked. "Yes, you can thank the outfit, I think. All that black and lace really lends itself to a more apparitional form."

"I completely agree," my mother said. She seemed to have recovered from my surprise siphoning act.

I stifled a groan. "Not that. How to defeat the pod demons."

"She means how to defeat the pod demons," Neville repeated for my mother's benefit.

"You've already uprooted the plants and destroyed them," my mother said. "Isn't that enough?"

"I have to take them out by root *and* stem," I said, remembering Demon Corinne's words. "The pod plants are the roots. Now we have to take care of the metaphorical stems."

"You can't kill any of those people, Eden," Neville said. "They'd be lost to us forever."

"I know *they* would, but I won't."

Neville stood silently for a beat. "You think one will be enough?"

"Now that the pods have been destroyed, yes," I said. "They can't generate any more spores. The only connection now is through the demons walking around. A network."

"Like the cloud," he said, more to himself.

"The cloud?" my mother asked, instinctively looking skyward.

"Cloud computing," Neville said. "Where you store and access data online instead of on your computer's hard drive. Agent Fury just wiped out the hard drive. The inhabited bodies are the network."

My mother pursed her lips, confused. "I thought you two weren't actually in the cyber crime division."

"It's not a perfect analogy, but it's the best I've got," I said. "Hopefully, everyone will be strong enough to reclaim their original forms once the bodies have been vacated."

Neville looked at me. "How do you propose to handle this when you don't currently occupy your own body?"

"I have a plan."

He pushed his glasses back to the bridge of his nose. "Do you need me to help execute it?"

"Execute?" my mother asked, her eyes shining with excitement. "Who are we executing?"

I gave him a solemn look. "Always."

CHAPTER EIGHTEEN

NEVILLE and I waited at a safe distance while my mother, Demon Me, and Aunt Thora prepared the Day of Darkness ritual at the vortex. As long as my mother didn't slip and say something to alert Grandma, the plan should work. She'd confided in Aunt Thora so that my great-aunt wasn't shocked by what was to come next. If Demon Corinne was willing to do magic to protect the pods, I could only imagine what Demon Grandma would be capable of.

"Look on the bright side," Neville said. "You're getting out of participating this year."

I glared at him. "Forgive me if I don't really see a bright side to this day." Especially if it was my last. There was always that chance. We had powers, but we weren't infallible.

Neville held up binoculars. "I see the dagger."

"I hate that dagger," I said. The bejeweled dagger had been in our family for centuries and was always used in the Day of Darkness ritual. To the wicked witches, it represented ceremony and tradition. To me, it represented blood and destruction.

"You'll hate it even more soon enough," he said.

I cringed at the thought. It was a good plan, if it worked.

"Can we trust that your mother has altered the ritual?" Neville asked.

"We can hope," I said, "She wants Grandma back. She'd miss the barbed comments and constant criticism."

"A strange thing to miss."

"They're strange women."

"What if your grandmother notices the changes to the ritual?" Neville asked. He was clearly growing anxious the closer we got to the pivotal moment. I don't know why he was so nervous when I was the one about to die.

"We'll cross that bridge if we come to it," I said. "If Grandma and Demon Me stay inside the circle, we'll be fine." Demon Grandma needed to be there in order to lock in the rest of the demons via the network and prevent them from jumping to another host at the last second. Even one escapee meant failure. We couldn't afford the risk. That part was down to my mother and the ritual. Demon Me needed to stay in the circle so that I could carry out the rest of the plan.

"Waiting for the signal," Neville said. "Your mother has just sliced all three palms." He paused. "That seems like a lot of blood. Do they always use that much in a ritual? I'm surprised no one ever passes out."

"Please stop the running commentary," I said. "You're making me nervous."

He continued to watch the scene unfold through the binoculars. "Between your family's magic and the vortex, this is your best chance."

I didn't disagree, but it didn't make me any less scared. What if I failed? It wasn't just my own fate I was sealing. It was everyone's.

Demon Me stood in the ritual circle, facing my direction, flanked by my mother and Aunt Thora. It was exactly where

I needed the demon to be. Even in my astral form, I could feel the powerful pulses of energy emanating from there.

"Go!" Neville barked.

I raced toward Demon Me without breaking stride. I ran straight into my physical form and pushed with all my strength, feeling the demon's resistance every inch of the way.

Get! Out! I insisted.

With one last push, I was back in the saddle. Well, more like sharing a saddle with my identical twin, but we wouldn't be uncomfortable for long if my plan worked.

I saw the dagger in my mother's hand, already steeped in blood. "I'm here!"

My mother didn't hesitate. She tossed the dagger to me and I snatched it out of the air before Demon Me or Grandma could react. I clutched the dagger and felt the magic throbbing beneath my fingers. A supernatural death would mean a supernatural revival for me.

I hoped.

It was now or never. My mother held Grandma firmly in place while I sliced open my arm from elbow to wrist. The goal was to make this as quick and painless as possible. It was only after I pierced my skin with the blade and felt the pod demon's life force ebb that I heard his voice calling frantically.

Chief Fox.

Was I hallucinating?

No, he was there, coming toward the vortex. *Great balls of fury.* He could see us.

I staggered to the ground and he yelled with such primal force that my bones rattled at the sound of my name. I dropped to the ground, trying not to fight the pain. Trying not to resist death. No matter how many times I'd been killed by my family, it had never felt quite like this.

And that worried me.

It was too late now, though. I could only hope that even if I failed to survive, the pod demons wouldn't. One sacrifice for the sake of many? I could live with that. It was my job to serve and protect the residents of Chipping Cheddar and I was very good at my job.

"Why are you all standing there?" the chief bellowed. "Why is there so much blood?"

Although their images were hazy, I could see my mother and Aunt Thora arguing with Neville.

"I thought you cloaked it," I heard Neville say.

"Why would I bother to cloak it when you could have done it?" my mother shot back.

Apparently, we'd been too distracted by our plan to assign cloaking duties.

"I don't know what you're arguing about, but stop right now," the chief said. "She's hurt." The pain in his voice was palpable.

"It's okay," I whispered, but I wasn't sure whether I'd actually made any sound.

"Eden." The next thing I knew, the chief was cradling my head in his lap. His tears slid from the scruff on his chin, past the dimple I adored, and landed on my cheek. I didn't have the strength to wipe them away. Too weak.

"Sorry," I murmured.

"Eden, don't leave," he whispered. "Stay with me. Please." He held me against his chest and the last sound I heard was the brutal pounding of his heart.

And then I was gone.

"Eden!" Someone slapped my cheek. Hard.

"Ouch!" I rubbed the sore spot on my skin. "Who did that?"

"Does it really matter? You're alive now. That's what counts." My mother loomed over me, flanked by Grandma and Aunt Thora.

"Did it work?" I asked. My gaze flickered to Grandma.

"Surprisingly, you managed to accomplish something," Grandma said. "Somebody schedule a parade."

Relief washed over me. Grandma was no longer occupied.

"Well done, Eden," Aunt Thora said. "It took a lot of courage to do what you did."

"Oh, please," my mother said dismissively. "Marrying her father took more courage than that."

"Mom," I said. "I'm barely back in the land of the living. Can you wait to slam Dad when I'm feeling better?"

"I have a nice glass of lemonade waiting for you in the kitchen," Aunt Thora said.

"I'm always thirsty after a resurrection," my mother said. "I think it's something to do with salt. That's why I like a nice margarita with salt around the rim." She sighed. "Now I want a margarita and I haven't even died today."

"I prefer orange Gatorade," Grandma said. "Replaces the electrolytes."

My mother urged me to sit up. "Let's take the photo again while you're still dressed appropriately."

My head was still murky with yesterday's memories. "Photo? What are you talking about?"

"Our Day of Darkness photo," my mother replied.

I struggled to sit up. "Didn't you take that yesterday?"

"Well, yes," my mother said, "but that wasn't really you and Grandma was on ice. We need to take it again."

"I am *not* posing for a picture," I insisted. "I just came back to life for Hecate's sake."

"I'll wait for you to brush your hair and teeth," she huffed. "I'm not a complete monster."

"I beg to differ," I murmured. My head throbbed as I made an effort to stand. "Did resurrection always hurt this much?"

"You're out of practice," Grandma said.

"That's a good thing," I said. "No one should ever have to get used to death."

"Hey, if you didn't have our wicked blood coursing through those holier-than-thou veins of yours, you wouldn't have been able to save the town." My mother fluffed her hair as though she was personally responsible for my DNA. Hmm. I guess she kind of was.

"Speaking of wicked blood," Grandma said. "Any fury powers?" She peered into my left eye and then my right one. "Flames are still there. How about the wings? Remove the cloaking spell so I can see."

"I don't lose the powers when I use dark magic," I said. "I gain them." My heart skipped a beat. "Do I look the same?"

"Unfortunately, yes," my mother said.

I touched various parts of my body to see whether anything new had sprouted. There had to be a fury power lurking.

"Really, you should thank us," my mother said. "If we hadn't killed you the last time, you wouldn't have thought of killing yourself now."

"We inspired you," Grandma added.

"You *murdered* me."

"I think I should join the FBM," my mother said. "It doesn't seem that difficult."

"You can't even open a jar of mayo without help," I said.

"Why exert the energy when there's someone with fatter hands to do it for you?" she replied.

I bristled. "My hands are *not* fat."

"Sorry, I meant big boned," my mother said.

"So everything's back to normal?" I asked. "The demons are gone?"

"Yep," Grandma said. "Demons are gone. Nobody remembers that anything strange happened to them. It's like another day."

Aunt Thora licked her lips. "Well, there's the problem of the chief. Nothing happened to him, but he certainly saw something he won't likely forget. He was so confused."

Memories of the chief flooded my head. His look of pure anguish would haunt me for years to come.

"He wasn't supposed to see me kill myself," I said. "I don't know why he was there."

"What do you intend to tell him?" Grandma asked.

"You can act like a ghost," my mother said. "Anytime he's around, you just make haunting noises." She proceeded to do a poor imitation of a ghost.

Alice stuck her head out of a wall. "How insulting. That sounds nothing like me." Her head quickly disappeared.

"Tell him it was a mistake and that you didn't actually die," Grandma said.

"He was there, Grandma. He saw me bleed out with his own two eyes."

"He didn't see where you went afterward," my mother said. "We basically shoved him out of the way and told him we were rushing you to the hospital."

"Just because he believed you couldn't survive a wound like that doesn't make it true," Grandma added.

"He can check hospital records," I said. "He'll know I wasn't treated."

"You have a sister-in-law for a doctor," my mother said matter-of-factly. "Verity treated the wound at home."

"There was blood everywhere," I said. "We were dressed like we escaped from a Spanish insane asylum in the 1800's."

"I honestly don't think he noticed," my mother said. "All he saw was you. It was quite touching, really."

"You can't tell him what happened," Grandma said. "We need to make him a Forget potion. You bring it to him when you tell him you're alive."

I needed to mull it over. Lies begat lies and I hated it, at least where the chief was concerned. He could be an ally if we let him.

"I need to make a few calls," I said.

"To the chief?" Aunt Thora asked.

"That's not a good idea, Eden," my mother said. "You're still woozy and likely to make foolish decisions."

"No, that's you after too many margaritas," Grandma shot back.

"These calls are work-related." I glanced around helplessly. "Where's my phone?"

"I'm not sure," my mother said. "Where did we put Eden's phone? Did someone charge it while she was dead?"

I zeroed in on Grandma, who was biting her lip. "Grandma, where's my phone?"

"It's downstairs. I may have downloaded an app on it."

"Which app?" I asked.

"It's just Little Critters," she said. "No big deal."

"Why would you download an app on my phone when you can play on your own?" I asked.

"Because I want to start over again with a new account and see if I can beat myself. No one else seems up to the task."

"Grandma, I use that phone for work. You can't use it to play games."

"What? I wasn't sure if you'd come back," she said. "It's been a while since you had to be resurrected."

"There was a chance your only granddaughter wouldn't

come back from the dead and your first thought was to open a Little Critters account on my phone?"

Grandma shrugged. "What can I say? It's addictive." She held out her hands. "And you're here now. All's well that end's well, right?"

I brushed past her. "I'm deleting it off my phone. No games allowed."

"No games, huh? Boy, Chief Fox dodged a bullet with you," she muttered.

I hurried downstairs and was intercepted by Princess Buttercup. The hellhound jumped up and landed a paw on each shoulder.

"Watch the flaming spittle," I warned. Her panting was enough to blow me backward. "I'm happy to see you, too."

She dropped her front paws back to the floor and trotted alongside me as I entered the kitchen. I found my phone on the island next to Candy. The cat spared me a look before offering a lazy hiss. She couldn't even be bothered to spite me properly.

I texted Clara to let her know I was okay in case she'd heard rumors, then sent Neville a message to meet me at the office. We'd have to file a report now that we'd taken care of the problem. No need to raze the town, thank the gods. Once again, crisis averted.

CHAPTER NINETEEN

I NABBED a parking spot right outside the office. "I'm alive *and* I got a good spot? Today must be my lucky day."

I opened the office door with ease, pleased to find that Neville's ward was down. If I didn't have to deal with wards for a while, I'd be a happy fury.

"Great infernal goddesses." Neville hurried to the door and embraced me before I could fully enter. "I was so relieved to hear from you." He continued to hold me a little too tightly.

"Having a little trouble breathing," I croaked.

He released me, pink-cheeked. "How inconsiderate. You've only just been reborn and here I am squeezing the life out of you."

"It's okay, Neville. I'm happy to be here, too." I went to my desk and my gaze landed on the sun lamp. Chief Fox's pained expression flashed in my mind again. I still had to decide what to do. I switched on the lamp and sat.

"I took the liberty of starting the report," he said. "Feel free to review and sign it." He gestured to the paperwork on his desk. "You'll be happy to know that I've received confirmation of Handel's extraction as well."

"Perfect, thanks." So Bruce Fendall had made good on his promise. That was great news. Handel wouldn't be allowed to set foot or distribute anything in this world ever again.

"I think this calls for a celebratory donut," Neville said. "My treat."

I rolled back my chair. "Why not? It isn't every day I come back to life." Then I would decide what to do about Chief Fox, after a nice sugar high.

We went next door to Holes, where Paige was busy selecting donuts behind the counter.

"Another bear claw, please," an elderly woman said. "I'm feeling hungry."

"Hi Mr. Riggin," I said to the old man beside her.

He turned to smile at me. "Agent Fury. What a nice surprise." He put an arm around the woman. "Shelley, this is Agent Fury."

"How are you feeling, Mrs. Riggin?" I asked. "I understand you've been unwell."

"Much better, thank you. It's like I've been asleep for a week. I feel like a new woman now, though."

"It's a miracle." Mr. Riggin inclined his head toward Paige. "We decided to treat ourselves."

"I usually make my own baked goods," Mrs. Riggin said. "Stuart insisted that we come here. I've been spending so much time in the house. It feels good to be out and about."

"I'm glad you're back to your old self," I said.

"I guess the doctors were right," Mr. Riggin said. "There wasn't anything wrong with her. I'm just grateful I have my Shelley back." He kissed the top of her head.

"Hey, there," Paige greeted us. "The usual for you, Neville?"

"I might try something new today," he said. "I feel like taking a chance."

"Wow, big day." Paige handed Mr. Riggin their big bag of bear claws and the elderly couple waved goodbye as they left the shop.

"I think I'll try your finest chocolate glazed donut, please," the wizard said.

Paige laughed. "They're all the same, Neville."

"One for me, too," I said. I wasn't about to turn down chocolate in any form.

As Paige retrieved the donuts, the bell above the door tinkled, alerting her to another customer. I turned with half a donut in my mouth and my heart stopped.

Chief Fox paused mid-stride and gaped at me. Although he wore his uniform, his face was unshaven and there were dark circles under his beautiful, sea-green eyes. I saw the rapid onslaught of emotions as he processed my appearance —shock, confusion, relief, and something else.

Neville plucked the donut from my mouth. I didn't know how to handle this. What do you say to the chief of police— to the guy you desperately want—when he discovers you're no longer dead? What does he say to you?

Apparently, the answer is nothing.

His long strides covered the shop in what seemed like a nanosecond. He gathered me in his arms and pressed his lips to mine, urgent and hungry. That single kiss sparked a raging inferno between us. He leaned into me as though trying to merge our bodies together. Forget resurrection—I never felt more alive. This moment—his reaction—changed every-thing. I couldn't lie to him anymore. Didn't want to. He was a strong man with a sharp mind and a kind heart. If anyone could handle the truth, it was Sawyer Fox.

"Oxygen, anyone?" I heard Neville say. He sounded so far away.

The chief buried his hands in my hair and leaned his forehead against mine. "I don't understand," he rasped. "I watched you die. I saw it. I checked your pulse. I even tried to resuscitate you. They took you away…They said to the hospital, but I checked…"

I slipped my hand into his and squeezed. "I'm okay."

"Why didn't you tell me?"

"You were next," I said. "I had work I needed to take care of first."

A strangled laugh escaped him. "Only you would consider eating a donut part of your job."

Paige set two cups of iced coffee on the counter. "You two seem like you need to cool down."

We broke apart, but he kept a grip of my hand, as though I might melt away. "Sorry about that, Paige," he said. "Agent Fury had fallen ill. I'm just relieved to see she's better."

"Shia hadn't been himself this week either," Paige said. "Seems back to normal today, though. He got mad when I asked him to mow the lawn. That's how I know."

Chief Fox didn't appear to be listening to Paige. He was staring at me intently. "Can we go somewhere and talk?"

"We are somewhere."

His gaze flickered to Neville and Paige. "Somewhere private."

"I'll enjoy my donut here," Neville said. "You go ahead to the office."

I faced my assistant. "Are you sure?" I asked. Neville knew what I was really asking.

The wizard clapped my shoulder. "Whatever you decide, I support you, O Immortal One."

The chief chuckled. "That should be your new nickname. Agent Impervious to Death Fury."

Oh, he had no idea.

"I think you might want a drink first," I said.

He glanced at the iced coffee. "I've got a drink."

"Something stronger," I said. In the immortal words of Grandma, sometimes you have to dispense with the looking and just leap.

"In that case, should we try The Cheese Wheel?" he asked.

"This isn't a conversation we can have in public," I said.

He pressed his lips to my forehead. "Good point. There are other things I'd like to do that can't be in public either or I'd have to arrest myself."

We left Holes and slipped back into my office. I locked the door behind us just to be on the safe side. Chief Fox didn't hesitate. His muscular arms reached for me and pulled me against his chest.

"Yesterday felt like a nightmare and today feels like a dream," he said softly. He kissed my forehead and then each cheek.

"What about Corinne?" I asked.

He rubbed the sides of my arms. "Corinne and I broke up last night."

My pulse began to race. "You did? When?"

"I'd left the hospital and gone home," he said. "I was obviously upset. Corinne came by to see me."

"Did she...feel okay?"

"She said she felt strange," the chief replied. "Like she'd blacked out. She asked me why I was...Anyway, I was choked up and said your name."

My throat tightened. "Did you tell her I was dead?"

"Didn't get the chance. She thought I was..." He looked away, suddenly embarrassed by the admission. "She thought I was crying over you. Over not being with you, so she broke up with me. Said that even casual wasn't going to work if I felt this strongly for you." He turned back to me. "And I do."

My head was spinning from the revelation. "Let's talk

first. You may change your mind about a few things afterward."

"Not about you," Chief Fox said. "When I thought I'd lost you…" He shook his head, unable to finish the thought.

"I'm so sorry I put you through that."

"It's not your fault," he said.

"Why were you there?" I asked.

"I was on patrol," he said. "Deputy Guthrie was supposed to take the park, but he's been…odd lately."

"Odder than usual, you mean."

"Speaking of odd, what was going on up there on the hill?" he asked. "There was blood everywhere. You cut your own arm with a dagger." He squeezed his eyes shut, as though trying to stop the memory from coming.

"That's part of what I need to tell you." My legs began to wobble. "I need to sit first. I still feel a little weak."

"Agent Fury admitting weakness?" He offered a wry smile. "Mark this day down."

"You'll be marking this day down for an entirely different reason soon enough." I sat in my chair and he perched on the edge of my desk. "There's a reason I'm alive today."

"Modern medicine is a miracle," he said. "Was it your sister-in-law?"

"No, it was my mother," I said. "And my great-aunt and my grandmother."

He frowned. "They're doctors, too?"

"No." I drew a deep breath. "They're witches." I'd leave out the wicked part for now. I didn't want to overwhelm him with details. "They practice…the kind of magic that can bring certain people back from the dead."

He laughed and nudged me with his foot. "Nice try, Fury."

I didn't smile. "You've seen these little flames in my eyes." I leaned forward and popped my eyes wide. "Do you know why I have them?"

"You said it's some kind of birthmark."

"No, it's an eternal flame," I said. "A sign of immortality."

His grin slowly melted away. "You're not making any sense. I think you might have a concussion."

I held up my arm for inspection. "Look. There's no evidence of a wound. I heal at a rapid rate."

He dragged a hand through his hair. "You're telling me that your family's a bunch of witches and that you're immortal."

"A coven."

"Excuse me?"

"Not a bunch of witches, a coven."

"You're going to get hung up on collective nouns at a time like this?" he asked in disbelief. "So why aren't you a witch?"

"Because I'm...something else." I averted my gaze.

"I know that much already," he said, his tone light.

I rubbed my sweaty palms on my thighs. "I'm a fury."

He squinted at me. "One of those kinky sex people that dresses up in animal costumes?"

"No, that's a furry," I said. "I'm a fury. An angry one. An infernal goddess. I don't work for the FBI. I work for a secret part of the organization known as the Federal Bureau of Magic."

He looked at me in silence for a long beat. "Does Neville know?" he finally asked.

"Of course. He's my assistant. He's also a wizard."

Chief Fox shifted off the desk and back to his feet. "You want me to believe there's an actual government agency dedicated to magic?"

"It's the truth. I don't know much about computers," I said. "It's only a cover."

He took a step backward. "I think you should see some-one. Maybe your sister-in-law can recommend a psychologist...."

"I don't need one, but I can see that you might," I said. My high spirits began to evaporate as I realized he wasn't going to embrace this revelation as easily as I'd hoped. What had I been thinking?

His gaze remained pinned on me. "Show me."

"Show you what?"

"I don't know. Anything."

I smiled. "Well, I just showed you I can be resurrected. Not just anyone can do that, you know."

His expression remained neutral. "Show me something else. Right here."

I rose to my feet. "Are you sure you want to see?"

He nodded.

I uncloaked my wings and unfurled them, my eyes never leaving his face. His lips parted slightly at the sight of the large, black feathers.

"You...You have wings."

"I do."

He remained rooted in place. "Can you fly?"

"Yes, but I'm not very good at it. I try not to use my powers."

"Why not?"

"Because then I get more." Fury powers were the gift that kept on giving.

He took a tentative step toward me. "You don't want more?"

"No, I hate them. I hate everything about what I am."

His fingers brushed the black feathers and then jerked back. "How can you hate something so amazing? So beautiful?"

"There's more, Chief," I said.

"Sawyer," he corrected me. "If we're going to be making out, you should at least call me by my name."

"Are we?" I asked. "Going to be making out?"

"Why wouldn't we?"

"Because I just blew your mind," I said.

"Eden, you blew my mind the moment I met you, and it had nothing to do with magic or fury powers or anything supernatural."

"I was drunk and mistook you for a stripper," I said. "If that blew your mind, then the bar's pretty low."

He chuckled and slipped an arm around my waist, careful to avoid the wings. "I can't claim to understand everything you're telling me right now, but I'm willing to try."

"You're not frightened?"

He stroked the wing with his free hand. "More awed than frightened. I mean, you weren't kidding about needing a drink for this conversation."

"You don't want to run for the hills?"

"Why run when you can fly?" he said. He cupped my face in his hands. "Are you sure you want to give us a try? What about the rules?"

I curled my fingers around his. "Let's say that death brings with it a little perspective."

"What other magic can you do?"

A hint of a smile played upon my lips. "Come closer and I'll show you."

* * *

Keep an eye out for the next book in the series!

ALSO BY ANNABEL CHASE

Thank you for reading *Bedtime Fury*! Sign up for my newsletter and receive a FREE Starry Hollow Witches short story— http://eepurl. com/ctYNzf. You can also like me on Facebook so you can find out about the next book before it's even available.

Other books by Annabel Chase include:

Starry Hollow Witches

Magic & Murder, Book 1

Magic & Mystery, Book 2

Magic & Mischief, Book 3

Magic & Mayhem, Book 4

Magic & Mercy, Book 5

Magic & Madness, Book 6

Magic & Malice, Book 7

Magic & Mythos, Book 8

Magic & Mishaps, Book 9

Spellbound Paranormal Cozy Mysteries

Curse the Day, Book 1

Doom and Broom, Book 2

Spell's Bells, Book 3

Lucky Charm, Book 4

Better Than Hex, Book 5

Cast Away, Book 6

A Touch of Magic, Book 7

A Drop in the Potion, Book 8

Hemlocked and Loaded, Book 9

All Spell Breaks Loose, Book 10

Spellbound Ever After

Crazy For Brew, Book 1

Lost That Coven Feeling, Book 2

Wands Upon A Time, Book 3

Charmed Offensive, Book 4

Made in the USA
Las Vegas, NV
09 May 2021

22718194R00120